BLACKBIRD

STONEWALL INN EDITIONS

Michael Denneny, General Editor

Buddies by Ethan Mordden
Joseph and The Old Man by Christopher Davis
Blackbird by Larry Duplechan
Gay Priest by Malcolm Boyd

BLACKBIRD

LARRY DUPLECHAN

ST. MARTIN'S PRESS/NEW YORK

Library of Congress Cataloging in Publication Data

Duplechan, Larry.
Blackbird.

I. Title.
PS3554.U55B56 1986   813'.54   86-13806
ISBN 0-312-08340-8
ISBN 0-312-00998-4 (Pbk.)
First Edition

10 9 8 7 6 5 4 3 2 1

LA-1993-1-49

To the Four of Us:
Chris and Wef, Greg and Larry
Ten more years!

ACKNOWLEDGMENTS

My sincere thanks to: Sasha Alyson, for publishing my first novel when no one else would; and for being so understanding about losing this one. Michael Denneny, my editor, for accepting this one. Deborah Daly and David Martin, for the beautiful cover. Daniel Knox, my official photog, for the pix. Bill Franklin at "In Style for Men," for publishing my pop music articles. Bry (the Welsh Witch) Myown, for her continued encouragement and criticism. Alan Esrock, for being my support group. Peter Kindem (the Incomparable Hunk of Funk), for friendship, good dinners, and free legal advice. Alfred O. Guzman, the high-school English teacher who encouraged me to write. Joan Robbins, the college English teacher who did likewise. Peter Thorslev, for teaching a Gay Literature course at U.C.L.A. in 1978 when no one else would. (God save the good teachers!) Michael ("Keep working!") Mahern, for giving my career new direction. Nadine Ciulla and Rick Hansen, for the best day gig I've ever had. Procter, who loves me long-distance. Thor Rodson, my first gay radical. Tom Richman, my first date. Ken Dawson, my first fan letter. Larry R., for the best 18th birthday present a kid ever got. Donn Weiss, for the U.C.L.A. Men's Glee Club, for some incredible brunches, for music that goes on forever. Bozine and the Bullets, Organized Rhyme, and the Dorian Men's Chorale, for music, brief but nonetheless sweet. Steiny, for good music, good food, countless additions to my slang lexicon, for loaning me gym shorts, and (hey!) for just being Steiny. Jeb, for all the love and laughter, for knowing it's wabbit season, and for calling me "Hemingway"—you *are* a Dahling! And (last but certainly not least) Greg, the best "author's wife" a guy could ask for.

BLACKBIRD

CHAPTER 1

I DREAMED I WAS DANCING THE waltz with Sal Mineo.

He was young, about the age when he did *Crime in the Streets*, which is about my age now. He was very beautiful, and about two inches shorter than me; and he smelled of Old Spice.

I remember feeling awkward, my feet unsure of which way to go. I kept saying, "But I don't know how to waltz."

And Sal Mineo said, "Don't worry; just follow me."

I woke up suddenly, as if awakened by a loud noise. My underpants were wet and sticky. And it was time to get up for school.

"Talent is beauty," Efrem was saying, just as Todd Waterson shouldered his way through the choir room's double doors. Which would have made a nice little cinematic segue, since Todd was not what I would call a major talent in any art form, but could have written the book on being beautiful. I thought of the juxtaposition of Efrem's remark and Todd's entrance in terms of film, both because I love movies and because last year, when Efrem signed my yearbook, he wrote "May your life be a movie in which you are Orson Welles: Write it—direct it—star in it."

I suppose I've almost always thought of my life as a movie, but since Efrem wrote that to me, even more so.

It was about fifteen minutes before first period, and Efrem and I were hanging around the choir room, something we did quite a bit. Lots of people do, since the choir room is one of the nicer rooms in the entire school, and since Mr. Elmgreen doesn't seem to mind if half the student body uses it as sort of a combination clubhouse and union hall before and after school and during lunch. Efrem wasn't even in choir, but many of the people who like to frequent the choir room aren't. We were straddling a couple of chairs up on the top tier of the room, up against the cupboards where Mr. Elmgreen stores the sheet music and percussion instruments and such. Just killing some time. Efrem was reading *Valley of the Dolls* for maybe the thirteenth time—it's his all-time favorite novel. The Foley twins were crouched into opposite corners of the room, plucking out a passable version of "Dueling Banjos" on guitars. There were maybe twenty or so other kids sitting around the room, reading or talking or strumming their guitars and singing softly to themselves.

I watched Todd clump-clump his way up the first tier, then the second, headed toward the back of the room; I must admit I was only half listening to what Efrem was saying. Todd was wearing his favorite pair of hand-tooled Tony Lama lizard-skin cowboy boots, with toes so pointy you could knit booties with them. And a pair of faded old Levi's hanging so low on his hips that his hip-bones were visible between the top of his pants and the bottom of his bright yellow HERE TODAY—GONE TO MAUI T-shirt. He looked hotter than a wood-pit barbeque. Todd was long-legged and bow-legged; and the way he walked in those boots and those Levi's, boys and girls, you best believe that was quite an eyeful. I have on more than one occasion followed Todd Waterson around school, ending up at a class I didn't even have, just watching him walk. I hate to use an expression as hackneyed as "poetry in motion," but that's exactly the expression that came to my mind every time I saw Todd walk.

(My own walk is, I fear, much more functional than decorative.

Marshall Two-Hawks MacNeill once described it as "somewhere between Bette Davis and Groucho Marx. Long, quick strides, face forward, eyes straight ahead, looking like somebody with someplace to *go*, by golly." But that was later.)

"After all," Efrem was saying, "time and gravity will sooner or later take its toll on even the most beautiful face and body; but talent—"

I'd heard this one before. It's one of Efrem's favorite subjects, probably because Efrem is under the mistaken impression that he's not very good-looking. Which he is. Besides, Efrem likes to use me as sort of a warm-up audience; he's perfecting his spiels in preparation for when he gets famous, so he repeats himself quite a bit. I fully expect someday to pick up the *New York Times Book Review* and read: "Efrem Zimbalist Johnson—Talent Is Beauty."

Efrem is a writer. I'm a singer. Anyway, I'm going to be.

Efrem Zimbalist Johnson is the closest thing to a real live Best Friend I've had since Martin Kirkland in the fourth grade. I feel a certain kinship toward Efrem, not the least reason being that we were both named after somebody famous. I was named after Johnnie Ray, the singer, whose biggest hit was "The Little White Cloud That Cried," back in 1951. Efrem was named, not after the granite-faced television actor most famous for his portrayal of Inspector What's-His-Name in "The F.B.I.," but after *that* Efrem Zimbalist's father, the great concert violinist. It was Efrem's father (from whom Efrem inherited his particular brand of pale-skinned brunet looks) who named him.

"I was expected to be," Efrem explained to me on more than one occasion, "the greatest American-born concert violinist this nation had ever seen. That was my father's dream for me. I hope," he would say, "I will not disappoint him too badly for becoming . . . the things I have become."

This was, of course, before what was later to become known (all-too-euphemistically, I'm afraid) as "the accident." It was after the accident, after his wounds had scabbed over (the visible ones, anyway), after much of his seemingly unflappable self-assurance and basic deep-down belief in his own superiority over most other mortals had returned to him that Efrem scrawled in the inside cover of my senior yearbook (in his inimitable ass-backwards southpaw writing):

To a Black Star (Young, Gifted, and Black—and That's a Fact!)
Love and kisses, Efrem.
A.K.A., the Divine Mr. J.

But I'm getting way ahead of myself again.

So Efrem is going full steam into his Talent-Is-Beauty sermonette, and Todd Waterson is toting his Ovation round-back acoustic guitar up the tiers. Todd wasn't in choir, either—he just liked to stow his guitar up on top of the back cupboards while he was in class, and he'd come in during lunch period and park in a corner and strum. Anyway, he's got the guitar in his right hand and his basic blue everybody's-got-one-just-like-it backpack full of books in his left, and (I immediately notice) he's not wearing any underwear. And his dick is quite discernable indeed plastered up against one side of the crotch of those jeans, and his balls are sort of bunched up on the other side; and I suppose I should have looked away immediately or at least tried to tune back into what Efrem was saying, but of course I didn't. And next thing you know I'm starting to get hard.

Which is not what you'd call a rare occurrence for me. Erection seems to be my middle name lately. I'll pop a class-A boner while reading anything even remotely sexual in a book (Efrem likes to read the juicier parts of *Valley of the Dolls* aloud, just to watch me get all hot and bothered); during just about any love scene in any movie; at the sight of a men's underwear ad (except the ones like J. C. Penney's, where the models' crotches have been airbrushed away); at the very thought of Skipper Harris, or (more recently) Marshall—but that comes later, as I said. And, as often as not, I'll get hard for no real reason at all, as if my dick just wants to let me know it's still there. And the sight of Todd Waterson's faded denim crotch (which, as he reached the upper tier of the room where Efrem and I sat, hovered dangerously at eye level) had me well on my way to a full-on throbber within mere fractions of a second. After attempting with some difficulty to cross my legs, I retrieved my three-ring binder from the floor beside my chair and plopped it onto my lap.

"How's it goin', Johnnie Ray?" Todd flipped his hair back as he reached us. Todd's hair was very blond and very straight and quite long in the front, so that an average of six thousand times a day his hair fell across one eye in an effect more than slightly reminiscent of Veronica Lake, and he would flip it back with a quick little backward neck motion. I generally dislike that particular habit, but on Todd it was really quite sexy.

"How's it goin', Todd?" I had only recently come to realize that the question *How's it going'* is entirely rhetorical. Time was when I would go into fifteen minutes on just how it really *was* going, causing more than one person to regard me as if I had taken leave of my senses.

"How's it goin', Efrem?" Todd made a modified hook-shot with his Ovation, landing it onto the top of the cupboard nearest Efrem.

"How's *what* goin', Todd?" Efrem rolled his eyes in that way he has when addressing someone he considers far beneath him—which is one long list, believe me. Efrem didn't like Todd very much. He said it was because Todd possessed the intellect of a staph infection, but I also think Efrem was more than a little bit jealous of Todd's looks. As I say, Efrem doesn't have the highest regard for his own looks, and Todd was practically a shoo-in for

Best-Looking of our graduating class. Who wouldn't be a little jealous? I was.

"You gonna audition today?" Todd asked me. Todd wasn't in Drama either, but he hung around the Drama room, too. Even though he wasn't particularly creative, I think he just liked to be around those of us who are. Or think we are.

"Uh-huh."

"You'll get a part," he said. "No sweat."

"Thanks. Wish I was as sure as you are."

"Yeah."

Yeah. Well, I never said Efrem didn't have a point—Todd wasn't exactly Mensa material. Efrem said he was only getting through high school on his pretty face, which may well have been true. Still, Todd Waterson was one extremely decorative dude. And, frankly, I've always been a sucker for good old skin-deep physical beauty. I mean, if I want scintillating conversation, I can watch *All About Eve*. Or, heaven knows, talk to Efrem.

"Well, good luck, anyhow," Todd said, making as if to leave.

"So how's Leslie?" I asked him, just to keep the conversation going for a moment longer while I enjoyed the view. Todd had been going steady with Leslie Crandall, the only daughter of our pastor over at the Baptist church, since roughly the dawn of time.

"She's fine," he said, just a little too quickly. I didn't quite know where it came from, but something told me Leslie wasn't exactly fine. Not fine at all. I wasn't sure if it was something in Todd's face, or his posture, or his voice, or the way he started fiddling with his pinky ring, turning it this way and that on his finger. Or what. It was just there, somehow.

That same something also told me now was not the time to pursue the matter. So I simply said, "I hope you're futzing around with that ring because you're about to give it to me." It got a smile. That ring never left Todd's finger, that I knew of. Leslie gave it to him. It's a beautiful piece, sterling silver with a big, shiny black opal, and I coveted it so openly that it had become sort of a running gag between Todd and me.

"I'll leave it to ya in my will," Todd said. Then he treated us to yet another vigorous hair-flip, and said, "Later, guys."

"Later, Todd," I said. Efrem kind of snorted. I watched Todd walk down to the doors, taking that incredible blue-denim behind with him. I'm telling you, talent or no talent, that walk was an art form unto itself.

"Well, I, for one, fail to fathom why you would even deign to speak to such as that," Efrem said in this very Katharine Hepburn attitude he likes to use when he's feeling particularly snotty.

"He's a nice guy," I said. I briefly considered adding something to the effect of, "Besides, it is my fervent desire to relieve Todd Waterson of his trousers"—but I didn't. About thirteen times a day I'd be that close to coming right out and saying something like that to Efrem. I was almost sure he knew, anyway; most days, I would have bet dollars to doorknobs that Efrem felt the same way about guys as I did. But for some reason, I always stopped just short of turning to Efrem and spilling the beans once and for all. I don't always make the wisest choices in life.

"He's a *mongoloid.*"

"He's a nice guy, Efrem, and not everybody can be the celebrated wit you are."

"Too true," Efrem said. "Too true." I swear, sometimes Efrem could be the most amazing snot. After a moment, he said, "Nervous about the auditions?"

"I dunno. A little nervous, I guess." I *was* a little nervous. God knows why. It wasn't as if I really gave a damn about the play. And I harbored no illusions about my chances of getting cast. It was just the sort of thing that made me nervous. Auditions, midterms and finals, interviews with my guidance counselor. Any situation where there's any kind of pressure on, and I get this rapid little tremor right in the center of my chest, along with an uncomfortable overfull feeling, like gas. I had it right then. And I knew I'd continue to have it all day, right through the auditions. I was definitely a little nervous.

"Whatever for?" Efrem said. "You're going to get a part. Heaven knows you're about the only person in the whole of what is laughingly called the Drama Department with even a *modi*cum of talent."

"Thank's a lot Efrem. You're a real prince." That was my favorite expression for awhile there: "You're a real prince." I'd just finished reading *The Catcher in the Rye* for Mr. Galvez's English 4 class, which, frankly, I wasn't all that wild about. The book, that is. I think Holden Caulfield was more than a bit whiny, what with all that dire teenage alienation schtick, constantly going on and on about how terribly alienated he was from everything. I mean, it's not as if *my* life has been this seventeen-year nonstop picnic in the park, but if I felt that alienated all the time, I'd just down a bottle of Sominex or fall on a samurai sword or something. It was quite dreary, if you want my opinion. It never fails to amaze me what kind of thing gets called a classic these days. Anyway, Caulfield has this habit (if you've read the book, you already know this) of saying to people (très très facetiously, of course) "You're a prince. You're a real prince." It was the only thing I really liked in the whole book.

"You're a real prince," I said to Efrem.

"You know I didn't mean it like that," he said. "I just meant you're one of the best actors in this school, for whatever that's worth, and that you really have no worries about getting a part in this overblown vaudeville skit Mr. Dead End Kid has decided to grace the stage with this semester, that's all."

Efrem likes to refer to Mr. Brock, the Drama teacher here, as Mr. Dead End Kid, because the most important thing in Brock's life (or so it seems to us) is that he used to be friends with Huntz Hall, who was in all the Dead End Kids movies back in the late

9

Thirties. Later he was with the East Side Kids, and still later with the Bowery Boys. Huntz Hall, that is, not Mr. Brock. As far as any of us knows, Brock himself has never done anything bigger than some summer stock in the Midwest somewhere back in the Fifties. He isn't even much of a drama coach, if you ask me. Efrem says those who can't do, teach; and those who can't teach, teach here.

Personally, I feel kinda sorry for old Brock. I mean, the man is sixty years old if he's a day. And sometimes I think, if I reach that age with nothing more to show for myself than having once palled around with some B-movie comedian—I mean, you should *see* the man sometimes, trying to make some meat-headed sophomore remember who Huntz Hall is ("*You* know! The goony one with the baseball cap!"). You'd think he'd get the message. But no. Just give him the slightest provocation, just mention the Thirties for heaven's sake, and old Brock'll jump right in with "Say, did I ever tell you I knew Huntz Hall personally?" When I told him once that I'd actually *seen Dead End*, it practically made his whole life worth living. It's kinda pitiful, I mean it.

"Let's get real, Efrem—I haven't got a prayer."

"What do you mean, you haven't got a prayer?" he said. "You were easily the best thing in *Thurber Carnival* last year. I said so, in print, as you recall." Efrem was entertainment editor of the school paper. "You did win last year's Thespian award, lest we forget."

"I know, I know," I said. "But *Thurber* was different. I did the unicorn-in-the-garden thing, and it was very cute and very, very safe. But this play is all about el-oh-vee-ee love, after all. And, being as there're no black girls in the department, if I did get cast, I'd undoubtedly have to nuzzle some little flower of white womanhood right there on the stage. I just don't know if this town's quite ready for that."

"Oh, come on," he said, "this is nineteen seventy-*four*. This is hardly the Old South, you know. We're not *that* far from L.A."

"We're far enough."

Efrem shrugged. "Too true."

Perhaps I should explain a couple of things before I go on.

First of all, this is a pretty conservative town—no two ways about that. It isn't very big, about thirty thousand people, and even though we're not even ninety miles from downtown L.A., it's still a small town in a lot of ways. There are a lot of Mormons here (who, in case you don't know any, aren't allowed to drink or smoke or do much of anything except get married and make a lot of babies and drink more Hawaiian Punch than you would ever believe possible); and those that aren't Mormons tend to be four-square Baptists like my mom and dad, and the Baptists are almost as bad off as the Mormons, except a few of them smoke, mostly on the sly. Which means certain things just aren't tolerated around here. Like, for instance, the plays done by our Drama department have to be edited—censored, really. All the Gods and Jesuses and sonofabitches have to be taken out, and all the Goddamns have to be changed to damn.

And there is a certain amount of racism here, too. I don't mean there's a lynching every Saturday night and KKK parades down the main drag or anything like that, but most of the black people live way out on the outskirts of town, either out on the Air Force base or near it. We don't, and neither does Cherie's family; but that's about it. Even in school, most of the black kids keep pretty much to themselves, and the white kids to themselves. So one thing and another, I thought it was safe to assume that my chances of getting a part in that semester's play were about a million to one.

The play itself was called *Hooray for Love*. It was a comedy revue—a History of Love through the Ages, or so it was subtitled. There was a takeoff on Adam and Eve, a scene about Captain Smith and Pocohantas, that sort of thing. All ending up with scenes of quote love in the Seventies unquote. Think of "Love American Style" in rerun, and you've got the general idea.

We in Drama II all thought the play sucked rocks, pure and simple. We had requested *The Skin of Our Teeth*, which of course got shot down immediately. So *Hooray for Love* we got. It was written by an old friend of Mr. Brock's (not, I hasten to add, Huntz Hall). And it was chock full of little huggies and kissies and just enough lame-o double entendres so that one or two of our more rabid Mormon citizens were likely to get their panties in a wad over it no matter who was cast. And right off the top of my head I could think of at least two sets of parents who would pull their daughters out of Drama (and maybe even out of school) if a young man of the colored persuasion was to touch them onstage.

So, anything Efrem might have attempted to the contrary, we both knew I really *didn't* have a prayer, and, frankly, the only good reason I could think of for going to the auditions at all was that Skipper would be there.

"I'm not intending to hurt myself about this thing, Efrem. You and I both know the play bites the big one. Besides, Brock'll probably make me student director as a consolation prize. And who knows? I might even swallow my considerable pride and do it." I did a big shrug.

"I still say you're wrong," Efrem said. "So where's Cherie? You always look so naked when you're not wearing her." At which point Cherie came in.

"As if on cue," Efrem said—which was exactly what I'd been thinking. Cherie bounced up the tiers, testing the dress code in a very short blue paisley dress—rather low-cut with a yoke effect at the bosom—which really showed off her breasts and legs. Cherie has these big legs, shapely but large, and truly impressive breasts— quite a handful if a guy's into breasts and legs. Not that she's fat, exactly, but she is rounded, if you get my drift. Cherie Baker will never be mistaken for a guy. She stood before me, brown and sweet as a Reese's Peanut-Butter Cup, a dimply smile on her full-moon face and a yellow rosebud extended to me in her right hand.

Cherie gave me a rose almost every morning—heaven only knows where she got them—just because I one day commented on the rosebud she was carrying with her through school. Roses are my favorite flower.

Cherie was also in love with me. So she gave me a rose almost every morning. And almost every morning, it made me feel a little bit sad.

"Morning, Johnnie Ray," Cherie said in that breathy, little-girl-lost voice of hers, a voice she seemed to have borrowed from Marilyn Monroe, a voice I was sure for the longest time just had to be a put-on. She slid into the chair nearest mine, scooting it as close to me as possible. Then she slipped her small, soft hands around my upper arm, gently at first, caressing my biceps; then she squeezed it hard for a moment, just before resting her cheek against my shoulder. All of which she accomplished in one smooth motion, while sucking in a long breath through her tiny, spaced teeth.

"Morning, Efrem," she whispered, as much into my shoulder as at Efrem.

She did this nearly every morning, too: the taking hold of my arm, and the long, hissing breath, as if the taking of my arm—an arm just recently beginning to show the effects of Coach New-comb's weight-training class—were a wonderful thing for her. And every time she did, it made me feel so sad. Sad for Cherie, for having the misfortune of loving me. Because I hated to see her tossing her love away. And sad for myself a little bit—being at least as much in love with Skipper Harris as Cherie was with me, I knew how it felt to love in vain. And I felt a little guilty, too, for not being able to love her the way she loved me. Guilty, even though I couldn't help it. Try as I might, the most that the touch of Cherie's impossibly soft flesh against mine, the baby smell of her fluffy Afro against my shoulder could elicit in me was the

completely irrational, totally unrealistic desire to protect her from all harm.

As if I could protect anybody from anything.

Come to think of it, the times when Cherie touched me were among the few times during the average day when it was reasonably certain that I would *not* get a hard-on.

At the time, Cherie was one of the two people who knew about me. Or, rather one of the two people whom I had told about me. I'd had to tell her; it was the only thing to do.

We met the first day she transferred here from Pittsburgh. Choir was about to start, and Cindy Metzler, the alto-section leader, approached me, steering another girl—Cherie—by the shoulders. Cindy introduced me as "our very best tenor," which, modesty aside, I guess I was. Now that I think of it, old Cindy was probably out on a match-making mission, and I was too dumb to notice.

"I'm not actually the best tenor," I said. "I'm just closest to the door." And Cherie smiled that smile of hers, full of sweetness and guilelessness and little baby teeth; and then she giggled, covering her mouth with her hand like a little girl. And she melted my heart. I think in my way I fell in love with her right then and there.

We were immediate friends. Cherie was enrolled not only in concert choir but also in the bonehead English class where I student-assisted—and in which Cherie sat behind me, often massaging my shoulders while I corrected spelling tests and sentence diagrams until Mr. Stebner said, "Cherie, I believe my assistant has work to do, and I know *you* do." Or something similar.

I knew Cherie had a crush on me—Stevie Wonder could see that—and while I did not encourage her attentions, neither did I slap her hands away or wear a T-shirt to school with Noli Me Tangere tie-dyed across the front. I'd be a liar if I said the attention wasn't nice; and in the absence of what I really wanted, the feeling of being admired, being wanted by someone as sweet as Cherie, made me feel good. It wasn't Skipper Harris by a long shot, but it was certainly better than nothing. And when people—Efrem included—began to assume that Cherie and I were an item, I did nothing to squelch the myth.

When she gave me the letter, though, I knew I couldn't stand to string her along anymore. Not that I'd ever led her on, exactly. Still, I hadn't felt completely honest with Cherie from the time I began to realize she wanted more than friendship from me—which was quite early on in the relationship. But I honestly hadn't realized just how serious Cherie was until she gave me the letter.

It was right after I'd told Skipper about me, about how I felt about him—which was easily within the top two stupid-assed-est things I have ever done—and which lowered me into a deep-blue funk the likes of which the world had rarely seen, for about two weeks. It was the first time I really understood the word heartbreak, because it honestly hurt so bad in my chest I could have sworn something in there had broken right in half. One night I lay in bed awake nearly till morning, just pounding my head with my fist and crying. It was a very bad time. And Efrem was all over me going whatsamatter whatsamatter whatsamatter, and I wasn't *about* to talk about it, but he just kept at me. But not Cherie.

She just stayed there by my side, attached to my right arm like a Band-Aid, pointedly not giving me the old wassamatta-you treatment. And then, two or three days into this deep-purple mood of mine, just before first period, Cherie hands me this big square pale-purple envelope, sealed. She kissed my face, and clip-clopped off to her first class (she was wearing a pair of those big clunky platform shoes). She had written on two pages of crisp paper the same color as the envelope; in pencil, in the erratic-looking little-kid writing I recognized from her spelling tests.

"I don't no whats the matter," it read, "but Id realy like to help."

Have I mentioned that Cherie is just about the worst English student who ever lived? Consistent D's on her tests, hasn't a clue about punctuation. Not that she's stupid, mind you; she simply has no written-language skills.

"Anything I can do Ill do," the letter continued. Cherie's particularly bad with apostrophes. "Just tell me what I can do."

Then came the part that really killed me:

"I offer you my love," it said, and the handwriting seemed to get even more jumpy than usual as she wrote, "I offer you my body, if that be your need."

That's when I knew I had to tell her.

I got myself to her English class early, and placed the letter on her desk. I had corrected the spelling and punctuation, and written on the bottom, "We have to talk."

When I told her, her face took on a very sad look, but just for a moment. "Are you sure?" she said. She sighed a little and said, "Just my luck, huh?" Then she took my arm like she always did, almost as if nothing at all had happened. And the subject very seldom came up again.

"Excited about the auditions?" Cherie asked.

"I haven't got a chance," I said—it was becoming a reflex.

"Don't say that," she said, her voice almost raising to ordinary conversational volume.

"All right, I won't say that." I raised a surrendering hand. "I sure would love to get my teeth into that Romeo and Juliet scene, though." The only thing in *Hooray for Love* that was even worth the bother was the first-act curtain scene, which was the balcony scene from *Romeo and Juliet*. I've always liked the play, loved the Zeffirelli movie, and I would have given both my chest hairs to play that scene. "Unfortunately, that would be about the last thing they'd let me do here."

"You don't know that." Cherie was about to really give me a talking to, I think, when Skipper came in—carrying his guitar, natch. In this town everybody and his dog has a guitar; even I have one. As Skipper entered, Cherie squeezed my arm a little harder, almost a reflex.

Skipper was wearing this ancient plaid wool shirt that he wears nearly every day of his life—it has this Playboy-bunny patch sewn to the left shoulder. He had his sleeves rolled up to his elbows, the shirt completely unbuttoned, with a tank top underneath. And I wanted to kiss his neck so bad. He tossed an eyebrow-flash up to where we were sitting and smiled, showing the two slightly over-sized canine teeth that made him look like a friendly vampire whenever he smiled.

"Hey, you guys." Skipper walked up and sat down just to one side of my feet and opened his guitar case, blissfully oblivious to the fact that it nearly wrecked me to have him so close.

"I woke up this morning with this song in my head, and I can't get it out," Skipper announced, ear-tuning his guitar, adjusting a couple of strings. I watched his hands plucking at the guitar strings, and I wanted to kiss his fingertips, stroke the backs of his hands. Funny thing: at one time I thought the worst thing that could happen to me would be if Skipper had decided we couldn't be friends anymore after I told him. But sometimes it seemed like this had to be worse.

"I need for you to do this song with me," Skipper said, inclining his head toward me, and sang, "Long ago, a young man sits, and plays his wait-ting game." His voice was soft and raspy, not really pretty—he's not a singer. I harmonized on the verses, and on the choruses, I came in on the obligato, the part Joni Mitchell sings on the record.

While we did the song, the room got about as quiet as the choir room ever gets. Even the Foleys stopped duelling. And when we finished, everybody applauded. Skipper smiled that crazy alley-cat smile of his and said, "Awrite!" and slapped me on the leg. And it hurt. Not that he'd hit me hard, of course. But I so wanted him to touch me, I mean *really* touch me. Like he touched Kathleen, when she let him. These slappings and punchings, these just-us-guys sort of touchings that Skipper liked to give me, this was worse than nothing.

"Gotta go." Skipper quickly repacked his guitar, stood up, and placed the guitar case on the cupboard next to Todd's. "I just had to do that song," he said. "See you at the auditions." And he bounded down the tiers and out the door.

And I thought, Shit, life really sucks sometimes. And I didn't realize I'd said "shit" out loud, except Cherie said "What?" And I said "Oh, nothing." And Cherie was about to say something when the Foleys came over, looking like Howdy Doody and his twin sister; each with a Fender six-string acoustic guitar hanging from their neck, looking (as always) as if they'd each been *born* with a Fender six-string acoustic guitar hanging from their neck.

And Johnny Foley says, "Johnnie Ray, let's do 'Judy Blue Eyes,' okay?"

"It's almost eight," I said, "I've got to get to French."

"Aw, c'mon," Janie said in that whiny little voice of hers, "you got plenny a time." And they kicked into the intro, and we sang. Johnny Foley on the bottom, Janie on top, and me in the middle. We'd gotten almost all the way through, when the warning bell rang, and we all lit out for class.

I PRETTY MUCH SLEEPWALKED through French; I spent most of the hour just staring out into deep space, thinking about Skipper, imagining reaching under his tank top and stroking his chest, and maintaining a pretty steady erection the whole time. I take to the French language pretty easily, probably because of my French blood; anyway, it's my easiest class. Madame Fournier loves my accent and, I think, just likes pronouncing my name with all the Frenchiosity at her command (just rolling the "R" all over the place), and for some reason she seems to think I'm the very cat's ass; so even if she catches me daydreaming (which she has a couple of times), she just smiles and says, "Dormez-vous, Monsieur Rousseau?"

When I got to the locker room to strip for second-period gym, I was eager for a workout, ready to work off some of the wild, caroming energy that was threatening to render me a blithering idiot before lunch. Gym has been just about my favorite class this year, which is quite an unusual statement for me, since I'm not what you'd call an athletic person. I have no interest whatsoever in team sports, and even less in the way of aptitude. Zip. Basically, I'd sooner be reading a good book.

This year, though, for the first time, they've offered a weight-training class (which I'm taking), and as I said, it's my favorite class. Both because I really like the effect that weight-lifting is having on my body, and because Coach Newcomb, who leads the class, is a total hunkus maximus. Big and blond and built-built-built. I fantasize about him quite a lot.

Anyway, I said my daily prayer at my gym locker that I not get a hard-on, with Danny Corson on one side of me picking underwear lint out of his foreskin and Joe Cjackowski on the other side bent over tying his shoelaces (he always puts his shoes on first). I mean, honestly, every day he stands there, bent way over, in nothing but his finely tailored birthday suit and his tennis shoes, and some days it just seems to take him for*ever* to get those things tied. And me trying to remember my locker combination and maybe even my name, thinking to myself, *Please* don't get hard. I've seen a couple of guys throw rods in the locker room, and believe me, there's no better way to get yourself razzed right out of school.

I threw myself onto the Universal Gym machine like a man possessed, in the hope that pushing myself to utter exhaustion might have a calming effect. I was doing my leg presses, and I was really into it, grunting on the push-out and clanking the weight stack when they hit bottom; and I must have been making something of a racket, because Coach Newcomb strolls over and says, "Hey, Rousseau— take it easy, huh? You're gonna hurt somebody."

Now, we have one of those old-fashioned leg-press machines that you practically lie down in and press the weight stacks straight up. I'd been lifting with my eyes closed, and when I opened them, I found myself staring right up Coach Newcomb's big legs, up the open legs of his white shorts, where I could see part of his jock. I got so hard so fast my dick nearly got a whiplash.

What I generally do when I throw a rod at an inconvenient moment (which, when you throw as many as I do, can average out to about every other one), what I do is I recite the Twenty-third Psalm to myself, very quickly. Usually, by "Thou preparest a table before me in the presence of mine enemies," I've gone down enough to where I can make a relatively graceful exit. So I started,

"The Lord is my shepherd I shall not want," closing my eyes again so as not to see Coach walking away (as the Coach is really something to behold, even from the back and even upside down); and I was okay by the time I got to "Yea, though I walk through the valley . . ." by which time George Watrous was standing over me saying, "Hey, Rousseau, you fallin' asleep down 'ere or what?"

A workout and a hot shower calmed me down some, but not much. I decided during my usual in-and-quickly-out, keeping-my-eyes-to-myself shower that I was in no shape to deal with Twentieth-Century American History, so I decided not to go.

I wasn't planning to ditch class, exactly. I am, I think I should mention, what they call here an Honor Scholar. The Honor Scholars program is one of the maybe three things in the whole school that makes any kind of sense. All it means is that if your GPA is three-five or better (I have a three-point-seven-five), they make you up a little laminated card with your picture on it, and they pretty much allow you to decide whether or not you need to go to a particular class or not. So if you've got some abominable Bio assignment and you feel it would be better for your overall educational life to work on that rather than go to English Lit and talk about *Ethan Frome* for the umpteenth time, the English teacher almost has no moral choice but to let you out of his class. Provided, of course, you don't start flunking out. It's a very nice deal as school goes. I mean, it's not as if you can leave school—ours is a closed, repeat, closed campus—and they don't particularly want to see you roaming aimlessly through the halls. Strictly speaking, you're supposed to go to the library or to study hall. But, after all, once you're there, nobody's breathing down your neck making sure you're doing what you said you were going to do. I usually read a novel or something, myself.

So I went down to Mr. Katz's room and told him I had this grisly English paper that had to get done today, and Katz said okay. Then I bopped on over to the library, flashed my Honor Scholar card, and made for the emptiest table, where Carolann Compton was hunched over some book or other. Carolann is pretty easy to spot, even across a room, since she has a veritable riot of naturally curly hair the color of new pennies. We're talking serious red hair. She was way over to one side of the table, and I was planning to sit way over to the other end and across from her. I whispered "Carolann," so as to ask her if I could share her table—just out of courtesy, of course, not as if she owned it or something—and she didn't seem to hear me, didn't look up, didn't budge.

"Carolann—" I attempted a louder stage whisper. I might as well have been talking to the table.

"Carol. Ann." I called her full-out, so of course both librarians looked up and glared a hole into me, and every living creature in the room turned to look, and finally Carolann looks up with this groggy, disoriented look on her face, as if I'd just awakened her from a hundred-year sleep, and says, "Oh. Hello, Johnnie Ray."

Now, a lot of people think of Carolann as a certified space cadet, but I'd always liked her. True, she did come off a little moody sometimes—some days she'd be very quiet and introverted, and other days she'd be smiling and joking and even a little bit foul-mouthed. And there were times, like this time, when it might take you two or three tries to get her attention, even if you were practically nose to nose with her. But, as I say, I liked her. She was different, and I like different.

"Mind if I sit over here?" I asked, rather wishing I'd just sat down, period.

"What? Oh. No. Go ahead." She looked back down into her book. Then back up. Her mouth opened as if to speak, and then closed again. And she looked back down into the book. Not the most normal behavior, I guess; but sort of par for the course with Carolann.

So I pulled out this short story I'd been working on for Mr. Galvez's class. I hadn't completely lied to Mr. Katz: I did have an English assignment, it just wasn't due for another four days. This

story was based on my experiences with Skipper. I was pretty sure
Mr. Galvez would be cool about it—he's cool about most things.
We'd been discussing the concepts of foreshadowing and symbolism in class, so I started out the story with a gray, cloudy morning and a single bird, all by itself on a telephone wire, singing all
alone. Which was to symbolize loneliness. I felt like Mr. Galvez
would get into it. So I'm just about to get back into writing this
story, when suddenly Carolann gets up out of her chair and plants
herself right across from me. And she gives out with this loud,
obvious "Ahem," just in case I hadn't noticed she was there, and
says, "Could I talk to you a minute?"

"Sure." I wasn't in the most conducive work mood, anyway.
And I got the feeling that this was something kind of important. I
don't know why. Just a feeling. Maybe it was the fact that Carolann's face was so flushed. She has that funny carnation-pink skin
like a lot of redheads have, and at this moment her face was so
blotchy and red you'd think somebody'd slapped her around a little.

"You're probably going to think this is really weird," she said.
"But I know you can handle it if you just keep an open mind. In
fact, you're maybe the only person in this whole school I would
ever dare talk to about this."

"About what?" It wasn't like the Carolann I knew to get this
mysterioso about things. Quiet, yes—but never cryptic.

"I need for you to promise me you won't repeat this." And I
thought, What is this, anyway? Just as I was going to mention how
silly this was quickly becoming, she said, "I know this seems silly.
Just humor me, okay? Promise."

"Of course," I said, not sure if I should be nervous or annoyed-
or what. "I promise."

"All right," she said, taking in a deep breath and squaring her
shoulders as if she were about to swim the English Channel or
something.

"Come on, Carolann, just spit it out."

"Well," she said, "first of all"—and she lowered her voice even further—"I'm not Carolann."

"Beg pardon?"

"I'm not Carolann," she repeated, slowly, as if that said it all and why wasn't I catching her drift? She just stared into me for a moment—waiting to see if I was getting it, maybe. Then she said, "I'm Crystal."

"Crystal."

"Uh-huh."

"You've changed your name."

She closed her eyes, pursed her lips, shook her head no, as if suddenly sorry she'd started this conversation. Which was pretty much my feeling at this point.

"Sometimes when you see me, you really *are* seeing me, and sometimes when you see me, you're really seeing Carolann."

"What?"

"No, wait, let me try that again. Sometimes," she said slowly, measuring her words, "when you see Carolann, you really *are* seeing Carolann. And sometimes, when you *think* it's Carolann, it's really me. Crystal. See?"

My mouth fell open. I was pretty sure I was beginning to see.

"You're dickin' me, right? This is a gag, right?" I knew this was no gag. Both because Carolann never joked that I knew of, and just because—well, I just knew.

"No. No joke."

"So, you're talking, like, split personality, right?"

Carolann, that is Crystal, nodded. "You're talking, like, 'Three Faces of Eve,' right?"

"Uh-huh."

"You're talking, like, your name is Crystal."

"That's right."

"Holy shit."

I dropped my face into my hands and just looked at her. This was a hot one.

"Then you believe me," she said.

"Sure." It never really occurred to me not to believe her.

"Oh, I'm so glad," she said, smiling broadly. "I knew you'd understand. I've always been pretty sure you were"—she looked toward the ceiling, searching for a word—"oh, I dunno—smart."

"Whoa, wait just a minute here. I said I believe you. I never said I understand. I mean, this is a whole new thing for me. Here I thought you were just moody, and come to find out you're schizophrenic."

"I am *not* schizophrenic," she hissed. I'd obviously stabbed a sore spot. "I am a victim of M.P.S., multiple personality syndrome, schizophrenia is an entirely different thing, look it up!"

"Hey, I'm sorry."

"No, I'm sorry. I just hate that word, that's all." She sighed a long one. "It's a long story. Basically—"

And suddenly a strange look crossed her face, as if she were having a dizzy spell. "Wait a minute," she said. "Carolann wants to talk to you."

Curiouser and curiouser. I looked around to see if anybody was listening in.

"Hi," she said as if seeing me for the first time that day.

"Carolann?"

"Uh-huh. Look, you're not going to blab this all over school, are you? I didn't want to tell anybody, but *she* just had to tell someone. You won't, will you? Blab, I mean."

"No," I said, even though I was already dying to tell Efrem everything. "I already told you—I mean, her. God, this is bizarre."

"All right, then. That's all I wanted to know. I'll let Crystal back out now." And she did that little dizzy thing again.

"We're back," she said.

"You were right. This is definitely weird."

"I know. But you can handle it. I know you can." She smiled a strange, equivocal sort of smile. "Anyway, I was about to explain."

And so she did. And what it boiled down to was this: Carolann's mother—her real mother, that is, she lives with foster parents now—her mother was deeply disturbed psychologically. Truly one step beyond. And she used to do incredibly cruel things to Carolann when she was just a tiny little girl. Beatings. Not spankings or even belt-whippings like Dad used to give me, but real beatings that left little Carolann black-and-blue and wondering what she could possibly have done to deserve all this. I could hardly believe it when Crystal told me about it. That anybody could be like that to a small, helpless child, especially their own. It's things like that that stopped me believing in God—but that's a whole other subject.

Anyway, Carolann's mother did all manner of terrible things to her. Locked her in closets for days at a time. Hung her upside down from the ceiling. So all of this left little Carolann so completely screwed up that her personality split. As an escape, her doctor says. In the wild hope that if her mother didn't like her as she was, maybe she'd be better off as somebody else.

"There were six of us for a while there," she said.

"Six?"

"Uh-huh. Let's see, there was me and Carolann and three other girls—um, Caroline, Annie, and I forget the other one's name; she wasn't with us for very long. And a little boy named Biff. But he wasn't around long, either."

"So there's just the two of you now?"

"Right. And Seymour, our doctor, he says soon it'll just be one of me again."

"Yeah? Who?"

"Who what?"

"Who's it gonna be? When you're just one person, I mean."

"Oh." She laughed a little. "Well, it's probably gonna be sort of a mixture of Carolann and me. But I'm trying to convince her to take my name. Crystal. Crystal Blue."

She studied my face for a moment. It must have been interesting reading at that point.

"You don't think I'm total Twilight Zone, do you?"

"I—" I wasn't quite sure what I thought just yet.

"I knew you didn't. I knew you were the right person to tell. Carolann wasn't sure, but I knew."

"Crystal?" I was sort of trying the name on for size. "How do I know which is which?"

"Well, that might be a little rough at first. I mean, we *are* sharing the same body, after all. But we're really different. We dress different. Like Carolann never wears jeans, and she likes those lacy pinafore sort of things that I wouldn't be caught dead in. And, well, we're just different, that's all. Once you've gotten used to the fact that there's two of us, you'll start to notice things."

I just sat for a minute, letting some of this stuff digest, before asking, "Whatever became of your mother?"

"She's dead," Crystal said, very quickly and evenly. "She hung herself in a closet a couple of years ago. She was between mental institutions at the time."

"Oh. I'm sorry."

She smiled with one side of her mouth.

"I'm not."

And I thought, Boy—this is gonna be some week.

CHAPTER
3

I SOMEHOW MANAGED TO GET through the rest of my morning classes—which, considering just how completely scattered my mind was after talking to Carolann and /or Crystal, was nothing short of miraculous. Lunch was almost as bad, because I was itching to tell Efrem about the whole Carolann thing, and I couldn't. I've been called a lot of things, but never a blabbermouth. So I just sat there on the whitewashed wooden porch of the Drama building, absently chewing one of Mom's meat-loaf sandwiches, thoughts weaving in and out of my head, with Efrem on one side of me reading Jacqueline Susann and making short work of a pepperbelly (which is a split-open bag of Fritos topped with chili and cheese—they're all the rage around here) and Cherie firmly attached on my other side, not eating— she was dieting, as usual. Skipper Harris and Paul Brecher were squatting on the other end of the porch, doing this Cheech and Chong routine for about the six-thousandth time:

"Hey man, it's me! Dave! Lemme in!"

"No, man, Dave's not here!"

"No, man, it's Dave!"

And so on. Not my personal idea of high comedy—give me *The Philadelphia Story* anytime—but Paul and Skipper (and a lot of other kids) obviously think these guys are just the limit, and so they've memorized all of Cheech and Chong's albums, and you can't get the two of them together without them kicking into one of these stoned-out comedy routines. Either that, or they'll go on for hours and hours about the Kennedy assassination—John Kennedy, that is—the Warren Commission, and how could Oswald have fired from that angle and the whole enchilada. And, frankly, given the choice, I'd just as soon have Cheech and Chong.

So I'm sitting there trying to eat, thinking about Carolann and watching (if not listening to) Skipper, who's wearing tennies with no socks, and I'm thinking, God Bless, even his *an*kles are sexy, when suddenly Cherie whispers, "I have to talk to you about something," in this way that I know means This Is Important.

So I said, "Alone?"

"Uh-huh."

So we get up and take a little walk behind the Drama bungalow, which is way out on the outskirts of the campus, past the football field—we often refer to it as the Leper Colony.

"I've been thinking," Cherie said.

"What about?"

"I think we should make love."

"Cherie, I believe we've been through this."

"Would you just hear me out, please?"

"All right." I stopped walking and we leaned up against the chain-link fence standing between us and the street. "Hearing you out."

"All right." Cherie crossed her arms over her bosom and stared straight out as if trying her best not to look at me. "You think you're gay."

"Cherie, I'm gay. Really."

"How do you know?" She turned and cocked her head to one side.

"I like guys, Cherie. I'm pretty sure that's the first warning sign."

"But you don't really know," she insisted.

"Of course I know, Cherie. I mean, this isn't something I just thought up this morning, like 'I think I'll wear my blue shirt, my white tennies, and oh yeah I think I'll be gay.' I know I'm gay, Cherie. All I'm waiting for is to get the hell out of this one-horse town and down to L.A., where I can go do something about it." I did a big shrug. "I'm gay, Cherie. Honest."

"Okay," she said, pointing her chubby forefinger at me, "but you've never made love with a guy, have you? You've never even made out with a guy, have you?"

"Cherie, I've never made love with anybody."

"Exactly. So how can you be sure?"

"Cherie—" I was trying not to become exasperated. I had a lot on my mind, and this was shaping up into one of the silliest conversations I could remember. "I don't have to make love with a guy to know that's what I want. And I don't have to make love with a girl to know that's just not for me."

"I disagree."

"All right then, disagree."

Suddenly, she slapped me hard on the arm, probably as hard as she could swing, because it really stung.

"Doggone it, what are you afraid of?" she said, her voice as loud as I'd ever heard it. "Afraid you'll like it?"

"God Bless America!" I rubbed the place where she'd slapped me. "What's gotten into you, anyway?"

"I'm sorry." Her voice softened again. "I love you," she almost whispered.

"I know." I took her into my arms and held her for a minute. How could I be sure, she says. Here I was with a pretty, sweet girl in my arms—a pretty, sweet girl with incredible boobs—and it was about as sexual as my meat-loaf sandwich. I got more excited looking at Skipper's ankles, for cying out loud.

"I can't turn my back on you two for a minute, can I?" It was Efrem. "C'mon back," he said. "I'm lonely." He smiled that great toothy smile of his and headed toward the bungalow.

I took Cherie's hand and started after him, but she stopped and held me up.

"I'm supposed to go visit my Aunt Lou Ella in Saugus with my folks this weekend. I'll tell them I'm not feeling well. We'll have the whole house to ourselves."

Her eyes looked so intense. I wondered if she had any idea how sad this was making me. She could have any guy she wanted, and here she was casting her pearls before—well, tossing herself at me this way.

And then I thought: Hey, what've I got to lose? I *was* a virgin, after all. I was pretty darn sure I really was gay, even without ever having touched a guy; but either way, I might just enjoy making love with Cherie. In my way, I did love her.

"Okay."

She squeezed my hand as we walked back to the bungalow.

Cherie insisted upon massaging my shoulders all through Mr. Stebner's class (while she was supposed to be separating subjects and predicates and I was supposed to be correcting sentence diagrams) over Mr. Stebner's periodic requests that she stop it—which, far from relaxing me, kept me as tense as ever. By the time I got to my own English class, my last class of the day (not counting Drama, which isn't much of a class), I don't think I'd ever been so glad to get to the end of a school day in my life. Here I had auditions coming up, I was planning to go to bed with Cherie Baker, and Carolann Compton was really two people. And it was only Monday.

Fortunately, Mr. Galvez had decided on a free-writing hour, something he does once or twice a week, where he brings in a record player and plays records—sometimes his choice, sometimes ours—and we just write. Anything we want. See, English 4 isn't required, so anybody who takes it is probably planning to major in English in college (like I am) or is at least more interested in the subject than the average. So Mr. Galvez seems to have a lot more respect for us than some of the other teachers do. Like, he doesn't take roll. And if we don't want to turn in what we write in free writing, we don't have to. All in all, Mr. Galvez is about the coolest teacher in the whole school.

Anyway, Mr. Galvez put on *The Joker*—Marcie Vandeventer had brought it in—and he sat and did some work or other at his desk, tapping his feet to the music while we wrote. I could hear his leg braces clicking a sort of counterpoint to the beat. Mr. Galvez had very severe polio as a child, so he has heavy metal braces on both legs. He still walks rather slowly and with what looks like some difficulty. Plus, he's only about five-foot-two, and wears glasses so thick his eyes look huge. But, you know, he's just about the cheeriest person I know. Best sense of humor. For instance, if you mention him by name in class, he'll say, "Please—you are speaking of the man I love."

While Steve Miller sang "I'm a joker, I'm a smoker, I'm a midnight toker" (with Mr. Galvez singing along, softly and just slightly off-key), I tried to work on my short story, but my mind kept wandering. Skipper and Cherie and Carolann and the auditions and then Skipper again. Finally, I wrote this little poem—about Skipper, naturally. It just came out, all at once. I never even erased a word.

And now
Once again
I see your beautiful
Funny face,
And your cartoon kitty-cat smile
Makes me smile . . .
Oh, my love,
If you knew how many times
I went to touch your hand,
Your hair,
But was afraid,
And didn't . . .

Not exactly "Dover Beach"—poetry is Efrem's thing, anyway—but I liked it. I even turned it in.

CHAPTER

4

THE AUDITIONS STARTED OUT pretty much as expected. *Hooray for Love* required a cast of eight—four guys and four girls—and considering there were probably six people in the Drama department with any talent at all, it wasn't too difficult to guess what the cast list would be before the auditions even began. For me, the hardest part of the whole thing was watching Skipper play with Kathleen Morgan all through it. Skipper had picked up this big white feather from somewhere—the props closet, most likely—and he was tickling Kathleen's face with it, tickling her neck. And she was giggling, and saying "Stop it, Skipper," and giggling, and it just about made me puke. I mean, as if it weren't enough just being totally nuts about Skipper and not having a Popsicle's chance in hell of ever getting my hands on him, without constantly having to witness the spectacle of Skipper falling all over Kathleen.

Did you ever notice how when you're lonely, it seems like the whole bloody world is suddenly determined to make sure you never for one minute forget how lonely you are? And I don't just mean the Skipper and Kathleen thing. You can't walk two steps on campus without tripping over a couple of kids rolling all over each other on one of the lawns, slurping up each other's lips like they were about to declare prohibition on smooching or something. Sometimes I'll see some couple just going at it like there's no to-morrow, and I feel so lonely and so jealous of them that it throws me into the most awful melancholy, and I could almost cry. And I feel like if I had the atom bomb, I'd just drop it right on these kids laying around sucking face, just so I don't have to friggin' *see* them.

Even some songs can make me feel like the loneliest man alive. "Killing Me Softly" is like that. I'm not even sure what it's about, but I swear, it just kills me. "Just Walk Away Renee" by the Four Tops—Boo-hoo City. "Popsicles and Icicles," by the Murmaids—every time those girls sing "these are a part of the boy I love," I get a feeling in the middle of my chest like a balloon inflating inside me, and I feel like if I don't find a guy to love me, I'll just, I don't know, explode.

Anyway, I sat there watching Skipper playing with Kathleen. Which for me was just about as healthy as using ant stakes for lollipops. But I watched them. It was like a car accident on the freeway: I couldn't seem to look away. And there was Cherie (a girl with absolutely no intention of auditioning herself, of course), clutching my arm and watching me watching Skipper.

And don't think I couldn't see the humor in all this, because I could. I mean, Kathleen was no more in love with Skipper than the man in the moon. She was just toying with him. He was never going to get anywhere with her, since she's a Mormon and is sav-ing herself for marriage, after which she'll have a litter of little Mormettes and be able to help create celestial kingdoms after she dies (I swear—she told me this herself). So there we sat in a little row: Cherie in love with me in love with Skipper in love with Kathleen in love with, I don't know, the Archangel Bony Moroni or something. Very *Midsummer Night's Dream*. And Efrem, our very own Rex Reed, who also showed up just to watch, sitting behind me and (I had no doubt) thinking "Lord, what fools!"

So first off, Brock has some of the real hopeless cases read, a few of the real no-talents with no chance of ever getting a part in anything. Then he had me read a scene with Jenny Borders—a mercy reading, I figured—something set in the Twenties, with a husband and wife, and the wife is going off to vote for the first time. It was a pretty lame scene, but Jenny's pretty good, and I think we read it well. Then Skipper, Kathleen, and Paul read the opening Adam and Eve scene, with Skipper playing the snake. He fluttered his tongue like a snake while he read, which was just about the sexiest thing I'd ever seen in my life.

After a few more readings, Brock had Skipper and Kathleen read the Romeo and Juliet scene, and it was direct from Puke City. Skipper and Kathleen are two of the most talented people in the department, but between making goo-goo eyes at each other and trying to come off like The Royal Shakespeare Company (doing these lame Diana-Rigg-in-the-Avengers British accents), they ended up looking like a couple of broken-down music-hall players. It was really quite embarrassing.

After they'd finished, Brock said, "Stay up, Kathleen. I want you to try the scene with Rooss." Meaning me. Brock always called me Rooss. Well, you could have knocked me over with Skipper's feather. Skipper smiled and said, "Show 'em how."

So up I went, and Kathleen looked almost as surprised as I was. I sort of shrugged, and gave her a "Well—here goes nothin'" look.

And so I launched into "But soft! What light through yonder window breaks," trying my best to make it sound as much as possible like a regular kid saying regular things. I didn't have to worry about the lines: I knew the scene pretty much by heart. Kathleen seemed to pick up on what I was doing right away—she's a pretty fair actress, as I've said—and she got into it, too. And the scene was good. Really good. I could feel it in my bones.

When we finished, both Kathleen and I laughed out loud it was so much fun, and everybody in the room applauded. Brock said, "Nice job." When I sat down, Cherie squeezed my arm and nearly smiled her lips off. Skipper turned to me and whispered, "Way to go, buddy. You're in like Flint."

I got home feeling pretty darn good about life. My showing at the auditions had me pretty cocky. Efrem had said that my reading was so good, Brock had almost no choice but to cast me. "Maybe," he said, "they'll just cut out some of the kissing and stuff." Why I actually let myself believe such a well-meaning crock, I shall never understand. I guess it wasn't until the reading that I'd let myself admit just how much I wanted to be in the show, to do that friggin' Shakespeare scene. I wanted it so much, in fact, that by the time I got home, I was actually convinced that I had a chance, a good chance.

I could smell Mom's sausage-and-rice cooking, which is one of my favorite foods. I could hear Walter Cronkite's voice coming from the den, so I knew Dad was becoming one with his favorite rocking chair and sucking up the evening news, full of President Nixon and Watergate and blah blah blah. Mom and Efrem's mom were in the kitchen talking; they've been best friends practically from the minute we moved here just over two years ago. Their voices sounded like a duet from some spoken operetta, Mrs. Johnson's soprano and Mom's low alto taking turns and overlapping.

I thought I heard Mom say the name Todd, and my ears pricked up. I walked into the kitchen and said, "Hi Mom Hi Mrs. Johnson," and both women clammed up and turned to me, coffee mugs halfway to lips, with these looks on their faces, almost guilty. And I knew something was up.

"What's going on?"

"Nothing is going on," Mom said in a tone of voice that was as good as telling me something was going on.

"Come on, Mom."

"If you don't mind, Shirley and I were discussing something that's none of your business."

"Clara," Mrs. Johnson said, finally putting her mug down on the kitchen table, "you might as well tell him. He's sure to hear about it at school tomorrow, anyway."

"Well, since you're sure to hear about it at school tomorrow anyway"—Mom sniffed a breath—"your friend Todd Waterson went and got the pastor's daughter pregnant."

So that's it, I thought. Why Todd seemed so strange this morning.

I said, "Todd's not exactly my friend, Mom." Which was true. Though heaven knows, I would have liked to be his friend. She just snorted, as if she knew I was hiding something. Mom has this funny attitude about kids my age. Somehow, whenever some kid in town does something wrong, she always acts as if every kid in town did it, including me. Especially me. "I guess they have to get married now," I said.

"Married?" By Mom's tone of voice, you'd have thought I'd suggested they jump off the top of the Empire State Building hand in hand.

"Yes, Mother. Married. You know—here comes the bride and all that."

"Now, don't get smart with me, Little Mister." Mom wagged a warning index finger at me. There was a Band-Aid on her fingertip from where she'd cut it while chopping okra for gumbo. It was all I could do not to laugh. Mom's about half a foot shorter than I am, Afro and all, and weighs about ninety-five pounds soaking wet, so whenever she tries to get tough with me, it's really kind of funny. I managed to say, "Sorry, Mom."

"All right, then. They're sending the girl away."

"Sending her away? I don't get it."

"Well, she obviously can't have the baby here," she said, as if that should have been obvious to any mongoloid.

"All right, I give up. Why can't she have it here?"

Mom rolled her eyes heavenward in this way she has that means "My dear, dear son—all that book learning, and not an ounce of common sense."

Finally she said, "Johnnie Ray, it's a disgrace."

"Aw, c'mon, Mom." It sounded a bit on the medieval side to me.

"She's the pastor's daughter, Johnnie Ray." Mrs. Johnson spoke halfway into her coffee mug. "It's a reflection on him." I don't know if I've mentioned this yet, but our family and the Bakers—Cherie's folks—are about the only black families who go to the basically white Baptist church. Most of the others go to the black church across town, but we'd just as soon go to church in the same neighborhood we live in.

"How can he be expected to lead the church if he can't even control his own daughter?" Mom said.

And I so wanted to say something real snotty, like "You'd think *he* was having Todd Waterson's baby"—but I didn't. I just said "I see," even though I didn't, exactly. And then, just as a semi-graceful segue, I said, "So what's for dinner?" Even though I knew.

"Sausage 'n' rice," Mom said, her face brightening once we'd moved over to a nice safe subject like food. "It'll be ready at six." Which is when we've had dinner every night for as long as I can remember.

"Well, then, I guess I'll go to my room. Nice to see you, Mrs. Johnson." Mrs. Johnson said "Nice to see you, Johnnie Ray," and I started toward my room.

I stopped at the living-room phone and looked up the Watersons' number in the church directory. I called and let it ring several times before hanging up. I don't even know what I would have said. Gee, kid, sorry your chick's knocked up?

The news about Todd and Leslie, and especially Mom and Mrs. Johnson's attitude, took a lot of the shine off my good mood about the auditions. I thought about the fact that if they, two of the less rabid adults in town, felt that way, there were probably people in the congregation who'd want to see Todd drawn and quartered as an example to all other horny teenagers, and pretty soon I was quite depressed.

I'm like that sometimes. Hearing about somebody else's troubles—Todd's or Efrem's or the starving children in Africa—I'll just get so depressed. Not all the time, of course, and not every bit of bad news I ever hear—heaven knows, a person could *stay* depressed. Just every now and then, I'll hear something—about some baby born with leukemia, or the number of times over we could kill every living soul on earth with our nuclear weapons or something—and I'll begin to feel like life just makes no sense at all. Just none at all.

And I'll want to cry like a baby, or break things. Usually, though, I'll just go to my room and listen to my stereo, a big old Magnavox mahogany cabinet model that Dad let me keep in my room after he finally broke down and bought a set of components for the living room.

So I went to my room, threw my books on the bed, and put *Court and Spark* on the turntable. I sat on the floor with my back up against the cabinet and let Joni's voice pour over me like cool honey. I figure, if you're going to be depressed anyway, you might as well listen to Joni Mitchell.

CHAPTER

5

I WAS ALMOST LATE TO SCHOOL the next day. Despite the fact that I woke up a full hour early, being so anxious about getting to school to check the bulletin board outside the Drama building. The reason why I was almost late was because I was locked in the bathroom jerking off. As I mentioned before, I get an awful lot of hard-ons, and a pretty good percentage of them seem to end up in my right hand. In other words, I jerk off quite a lot. Which bothers me sometimes, like maybe I do it too much. Johnnie Ray Rousseau, boy nympho—film at eleven. But, how much is too much? Twice a day? Five times? Ten? I'm sure Pastor Crandall would say that it's too much if you do it at all. And some days, I actually lose count. I'll do it in the morning before school in the bathroom, and at night against the sheets, maybe one or two quick ones in the head at school between classes. Sometimes, if I'm left alone in the house on a weekend or in the evening, I'll do it over and over, just to see how many times I can. One Saturday, I did it twenty-two times. I finally stopped for fear I might come blood or something.

Anyway, this morning I'd awakened from a delicious dream about me and Coach Newcomb—I always have my best dreams in the morning right before I wake up—and I continued the fantasy after my shower, sitting on the toilet seat. Coach is in just his jockstrap and I'm totally naked, and I'm standing right on his big bare feet and running my hands all over his body, and we're kiss-ing. And I'm really into this, stroking and stroking and licking and kissing at the air, when Mom knocks bum-bum-bum-BUM on the bathroom door.

"Johnnie Ray, you're gonna miss the bus if you don't hurry up."

"I'm hurrying, Mother."

"Well, you'd better just keep *on* hurrying. Honestly, Johnnie Ray, I just don't know what you could be *do*ing all that time in the bathroom. I swear, you take longer to get ready than *I* do." And her voice faded down the hall with the sound of her quick, pink-slippered footsteps. Sometimes I wonder if Mom really doesn't know what I do in the bathroom, or if she just pretends not to know.

Anyway, so I hurried it up. And Coach and I are really kissing now, and he's rubbing me up and down with his big hands, and just as I was getting really, really close, I hear Mom again, yelling from the kitchen,

"Johnnie Ray Rousseau, I want your black butt out of that bathroom, now! The bus is comin'!"

By which time the bus wasn't the only thing that was coming. I shot so hard it hit the opposite wall. I gathered myself together as fast as I could, wiped the sticky mess up off the wall, yanked up my Levi's, tucked in my T-shirt, patted my hair, and emerged from the bathroom with what I hoped was an air of collected cool.

Mom was waiting at the door with my sweatshirt, my backpack, and my lunch.

"Baby," she said, just dripping sarcasm, "I'm so glad you're all right. I thought maybe you'd gone and flushed yourself down the commode." Mom says I'm too sarcastic, which may be true, but let me tell you, I come by it honest.

"Très drôle, Mother; you really *must* go on the stage."

"I'll leave the play-actin' to you, Mister Smart-Ass. Let's see you play the part of watching the bus pulling down the street."

I looked out the kitchen window and saw the back of the bus chugging slowly away. And I said, "Aw, shit." Which was a serious slip. One thing Mom does not abide is any swearing.

"Johnnie Ray Rousseau, I will not have that kind of language used in my house, and you know it. I don't know what some people's mothers may put up with, and I don't care. As long as you're living under *my* roof—"

"Mom I'm sorry I gotta go I'm sorry it won't happen again bye, Mom." I kissed her on the cheek and bounded out the door like Arthur Lake in the Blondie movies. I lit out after the bus, the world-champion track star going for the gold, my book bag tucked under my arm and my lunch clutched in the other hand, my sneakers making a chip-chip-chip sound against the street as I ran.

I was pretty sure I could catch the bus at the next stop; I had to catch it or I'd be late. As I gained on the big, slow vehicle, I could see faces pressed against the back window of the bus, grinning and waving and cheering me on.

As I reached the exhaust-billowing tail end of the bus, I realized it was waiting for me. Bill the bus driver opened the doors and I climbed aboard, sweaty and huffing breaths. The kids on the bus applauded as Bill punched my bus card. Bill is one of the biggest, ugliest men I have ever seen—he had his four front upper teeth knocked out in some fight or other and never bothered to do anything about it—and he's also, I think, just slightly retarded. But also one of the most likable people in town. All the kids really dig the guy.

"Wayda go, champ!" Bill grinned his snaggle-toothed grin.

"Thank you all." I smiled and bowed, still out of breath but every inch a star. "You're much too kind. Ah, my public," I said, flopping into an empty seat near the back, "how they love me."

Just as I sat down, I heard someone call my name from behind me. I turned to see Carolann, or rather Crystal—at least I thought it was Crystal—sitting alone in the long seat at the very back of the bus. She motioned me over.

"Hi," I said, and sat down next to her, and then I whispered, "Crystal?" She smiled and nodded.

"It's so nice to be called by my own name," she said. "Gonna go check the bulletin board?"

"Yeah."

"Nervous?"

"Little bit." In fact, as soon as I sat down and began to catch my breath, I could feel that little tremor coming on, right on schedule. I was all but dead sure I was cast, but it didn't matter.

Crystal looked around the bus like a movie spy checking to see if the coast was clear. Then she leaned in close and whispered, "I've got something to tell you."

"Something else?"

"Uh-huh."

"Is it anything like what you told me yesterday?"

"No, not really," she said. "But it's sort of unusual, too." She was whispering, which was silly, noisy as it was on that bus.

"Crystal," I had to ask, "why me?"

"Because . . ." She shrugged. "I don't know," she said. "What I told you yesterday was because I wanted to tell you what I'm about to tell you now, and I didn't want to do it pretending to be Carolann."

"Huh?"

"Never mind," she said, and she reached into her purse (this enormous old macramé monstrosity that she no doubt made herself—I've made better ones myself) and pulled out a deck of cards. "Here," she said, handing me the deck. "Shuffle these."

"This is what you had to tell me? That you're heavily into pinochle?"

"You're really nervous," she said. "You always joke when you're nervous, don't you?" Matter of fact, I do. I shuffled the cards.

"Okay," I said. "So I've shuffled the cards. So what?"

"The top card is the jack of diamonds," she said.

"What?"

"Jack of diamonds," she repeated. "Turn it over." I did. And it was.

"Three of spades," she said. Right again.

And again. And again. And again.

I believe she missed two out of the fifty-two.

"I don't suppose this is some clever illusion," I said. I knew it wasn't.

"Nope."

"You're psychic."

"Uh-huh." She took the cards from me and began to shuffle them. "Wanna see me do it again? I usually get them all."

"No, that's okay. I'm sure you'd get it this time. You're just full of surprises, aren't you?"

She smiled.

"Is that it?" I asked her. "Just the card thing?"

"Oh, no," she said. "I know when the phone's gonna ring before it does; I know when somebody's gonna come over, even if they haven't said so. That sort of thing. I'm slightly psychokinetic: I can move things, small things, nothing heavy and not very far. A couple of years ago, though, I had what they used to call poltergeist. Things used to fly around my room—dolls, teddy bears, perfume bottles. I couldn't control it."

"Do you read minds? Like do you know what I'm thinking?"

"Not really read minds. I mean, not word for word, like a textbook or something. But I can usually sense the general gist—like right now you're not sure whether or not you believe me." She was right about that.

"Do you know if I got a part in the show?"

She laughed.

"No, I can't see the future. I don't have a crystal ball, either."

"Have you done this—had this—all your life?"

"As far as I can remember."

"What about Carolann?"

"She doesn't have any psychic powers to speak of, as far as we can tell."

"Look, Crystal, it's not like this isn't interesting and all, because it is. But I'm still not sure why you're letting me in on all this."

"Well, like I said yesterday, I wanted to tell somebody. Some days I feel like I'm gonna burst if I don't tell somebody. And *you* know what I mean."

I felt a funny little quiver when she said that. Like she knew something.

"And," she continued, "I had a feeling you could deal with it. Besides, I think you might have it, too." She finished with a little nod of her head.

"Who, me?"

"Uh-huh."

"What makes you think that?"

"I don't know," she said, "it's just a feeling. Listen: Don't you sometimes feel like you know just what a person's really feeling, even if they're saying something else?"

"Well, sure, but—"

"And I bet you have really strong hunches, like intuition. Like you have a feeling about something, and later you find out you were right. Right?"

"Right."

"See, I can tell you're a very sensitive person. And that's all ESP really is; it's just heightened sensitivity. And you're a lot more sensitive than most guys. Than most girls, even. Maybe it has something to do with your being gay."

I swear, my heart stopped for a second. I looked around the bus really fast, wondering if anybody had heard her.

"God bless it! Who told you that?" I couldn't believe Cherie would have told anybody, and Skipper had sworn he wouldn't.

"Nobody *told* me," Crystal said, a little satisfied smile on her face. "I just know. I only mentioned it to get your attention. Worked, didn't it?"

"All right, so it worked. And what else do you know?"

"I know you're strung out over Skipper Harris." My mouth must have fallen open a mile. Crystal shrugged. "You don't have to be psychic to figure that one out. Just observant."

"Shit."

"Don't worry. I'm not going to blab it all over town or anything. After all, it's not as if you don't have the goods on me, right? Anyway, the point is I think you've got it, too."

"Got what, too?" I was stalled back at "something to do with your being gay."

"ESP, of course."

"I don't know, Crystal. Hunches and stuff are one thing, but it's not as if I'm forever moving things with my mind or anything."

"I'm telling you you've got the basic power—maybe not as much as me, but I know you've got it. Almost everybody has some, and you've got more than the average, I'm sure of it. It's just a matter of exercising it. Building it up. Like those arms of yours." She took a playful poke at my biceps.

"Look," she said, "why doncha just try the cards, okay?" She gave the deck a quick shuffle. "Don't go for the suits or anything yet—just black or red."

And I thought, what have I got to lose?

Well, the upshot is that I got better than half of them right, but I know enough about averages to know that didn't mean diddly.

"Not statistically significant," Crystal said, slipping the deck back into its box. "But, after all, we are on a bus full of people, and your mind's distracted—I could tell that, it's like a mob scene in there." She tapped the top of my head. By this point, the bus was pulling into school.

"Are you gonna do independent study third period today?" she asked.

"I could."

"Good. I'll meet you in the library, then. Much better atmosphere. If Carolann's there, just ask for me." She tucked the cards back into her purse, and the thought crossed my mind that it might be a trick deck.

"You can bring your own deck tomorrow," Crystal said, a rather smug little smile on her face, which immediately made me feel like a fool just for thinking it.

We got off the bus, and I waved over my shoulder at Crystal and quick-stepped across campus toward the Drama bungalow, my chest gulping breaths, my head nearly bursting with thoughts and eagerness and anxiety. Mornings tend to be cold here, even in the spring. The morning air was icy (and so was the grass: it crunched softly beneath my sneakers as I crossed the football field, like walking on Rice Krispies); it made my chest hurt just to breathe. I pulled the hood of my sweatshirt over my head and pulled the drawstrings tight around my face.

As I approached the bungalow, I could see Skipper standing to one side of it, reading the cast list. He was the only person there. By the time I reached the building, Skipper had turned away from the bulletin board. When he saw me, his face fell halfway to the ground; then he forced his lips to smile, and waved in my direction.

"Hey, buddy," he called to me. He jerked his head toward the board. "Just readin' the body count."

And I knew. I hadn't been cast. I knew it as surely as I knew it was Tuesday morning and my name was Rousseau and it was cold outside. Even before Skipper said, "Hey, buddy, I'm real sorry.

You should have been cast. You gave the best reading of anybody. Everybody knows that." Skipper put a hand on my shoulder.

"Yeah, well"—I did my best what-the-hey shrug—"I guess—" And my voice broke, and my eyes pitched a short fit of blinking. Skipper, obviously at a loss for what to do in the extremely probable event that I started crying, took this as his cue to skiddoo.

"I gotta go, buddy. I'm real sorry. I'll see you in the choir room, okay?" he said real fast, and hurried away from me, his feet crunching against the icy grass on the football field.

Finally, I looked up at the cast sheet. I checked the bottom of the list first. Lo and behold, there it was: "Student director— Johnnie Ray Rousseau." Then I looked at the cast list itself. Jenny was cast. And Kathleen. Skipper, of course, and Paul. When I saw the names of the other two guys, I couldn't believe it. Les Needels and Carter Murphree. Carter Murphree, who'd given one of the worst auditions in the history of the theater. Who couldn't act his way out of a wet paper bag.

Suddenly, I felt something go twang inside me. It seemed nearly audible, like the harp string that breaks in *The Cherry Orchard*. I began to tremble from head to foot, and it wasn't from the cold.

It was one of those times when my life seemed most like a movie. Only I was neither the writer nor the director of this scene. I was the actor, and, strangely, the audience. I watched with a mixture of surprise and calm as I marched up the wooden steps of the bungalow and threw open the door with such force that it flew to the wall and locked wide open against its doorstop.

"Goddamn you, Brock!" I yelled in a voice I hardly recognized.

Brock was seated at his desk at the front of the room, shuffling some paper. He looked up quickly, understandably startled.

"Rooss—"

"God-*damn* you, Brock!" It was all I could seem to come up with for a while there. As always seems to happen when I am truly furious, the tears came, coursing down my face, dripping down my neck and onto the front of my sweatshirt. I wiped at my eyes with the heels of my hands.

"Now, wait just a minute, Rooss." Brock made as if to get up out of his chair, but ended up in a funny-looking half-squat over it. "You know I could have you suspended for that sort of language."

"Is that so?" I was slipping into Bette Davis, really biting off my words. I crossed my arms over my chest and tapped my right foot feverishly against the floor. I snorted a quick breath. "Well, why don't you just *do* that, Mister Brock." This took him somewhat by surprise. I was not known for talking back to teachers, let alone swearing at them.

"You know I deserved a part in your goddamn play more than Carter Murphree did. You *know* it!"

"No, Rooss, I'm afraid I don't know that at all—"

"Shut up! You know it and I know it and everybody at the audition knows it. My audition was better than Carter's, and better than Skipper's. Better than anybody's!" I took in a couple of big, trembly breaths.

"This is a very subjective thing we're talking about here, Rooss. Besides, the audition isn't the whole story. There are other factors to be considered when casting a production."

"There's one reason and only one reason why I wasn't cast, and you know what it is as well as I do. Why couldn't you go against this goddamn town just once? Just once? 'Cause you're a goddamn racist, just like most of this town, that's why, you old—Why the hell couldn't you just—" And I was so angry and hurt and frustrated I thought I might throw a chair through a window or something, so I turned to leave. Then I whipped back around.

"And furthermore, you can take your goddamn student directorship and just sit on it and rotate! I wouldn't student direct if you *paid* me!" And I started down the stairs again. Stopped. Turned around and walked back to the door.

"And *further*more," I screamed, "I hated *Dead End*. It was the stupid-assed-est movie I ever *saw!*"

And I was out of there. Bat-out-of-hell material. My vision was blurred with tears, and I nearly knocked some kid down coming off the steps—maybe half a dozen kids had gathered while I was yelling.

I heard Efrem's voice call, "Hey, Johnnie Ray, wait up."

"Leave me alone," I yelled over my shoulder. And I hot-footed it across the football field, right through campus and out, and just kept on walking. I didn't even slow down till I got home.

"It's just me, Mom," I called. I could hear the television from the family room. Mom was ironing Dad's shirts and watching a "Big Valley" rerun. Mom's a big Stanwyck fan from way back.

"Boy, what in the world are you doing home?" Mom called from the other room. I could picture the iron poised over the board in mid-stroke.

"I wasn't feeling well, so I came home."

She must have broken the sound barrier getting to me. She was right in front of me in nothing flat, the back of her hand pressed against my forehead.

"What's the matter, Baby?" she said in the soft voice she uses less and less as I get older. "Your eyes are red, but you don't have a temp."

"Just a little sick to my stomach, Mom."

"Did you puke?"

"Uh-huh." I thought, why not go all the way.

"Well, you just take you some Pepto-Bismol and get right back in that bed, and in a little while I'll heat you up some soup."

And I said "Okay, Mom" and went to my room. I turned the

radio on and tuned it to this station way over to the left of the FM dial, where all they play, all day and all night, is a woman's voice reading numbers in French. Sometimes, when I'm really upset, I find it soothing.

After a while, I had to laugh a little at the spectacle I must have made of myself—talk about your Drama. I'd never said goddamn out loud before in my life. For a minute, I wondered if Brock might make good on his threat to have me suspended. He really could, after all: I had sworn at a teacher, even if it wasn't in class, exactly. But I was pretty sure he wouldn't. He's a pretty wormy old guy, and besides, I think deep down he knew he was wrong, both morally and artistically. Carter Murphree was bound to be incurably lame on stage.

I'm not sure how long I sat there listening to the French numbers and thinking, but after a while, Mom knocked on the door and peeked in.

"I thought you might be asleep," she said, half-whispering as if she had indeed awakened me. "You have a phone call," she said. "It's Cherie."

The way Mom smiled whenever she mentioned Cherie, or talked to her, I knew she took it for granted that Cherie was my girlfriend, and she liked it. From my freshman year on, Mom seemed worried that I wasn't dating. She'd been a real dater herself in high school.

"I heard what happened. I'm so sorry," Cherie said. Her powdery little voice was just barely audible against the surrounding noises—she was calling from a pay phone on campus.

"Thanks," I said, real sarcastic. So, of course I immediately felt like a raving shitheel. I really hate myself when I'm mean to Cherie—I mean, how could anybody be mean to someone like Cherie? But sometimes I just can't help it. It may come as a surprise to you, but relentless devotion can be absolutely annoying sometimes.

Cherie didn't say anything for a while. All I could hear was the background noise, a soft, steady whoosh almost like putting a sea-shell to your ear.

"Look," I finally said, "I really appreciate your calling, and I realize I'm being a real anus, and I'm sorry. I'm just in a real lousy mood right now, okay?"

"Okay."

"So I'll see you tomorrow, okay?"

She sighed an okay.

"Oh, yeah," she said. "I wanted to tell you something. Brock just posted this announcement about auditions over at the J.C. for some directing-students' projects. Some of them need high-school age people for their one-acts. It's tomorrow night. Maybe you should go."

In my present bitchy condition, I felt like Cherie was throwing me a bone (which she wasn't, of course) instead of being genuinely helpful (which she was).

"Thanks a lot, Cherie," I said, just oozing sarcasm. "I'll make sure to do that." And of course I instantly felt rotten for taking that tone with her again. "Look, I'll talk to you tomorrow. Bye."

And just as the receiver was about to hit the cradle, I just barely heard Cherie say "I love you." Which made me feel about as shitty as a guy should ever have to feel.

I just lay back on my bed with my arm across my eyes, clench-ing my fists until my forearms ached, and listened to French num-bers until Mom knocked on the door again and said, "Soup's ready."

CHAPTER
6

I LOOKED FOR CRYSTAL ON THE bus the next morning, but she wasn't on it. In the midst of my emotional fireworks display of the morning before, I had forgotten my date to meet Crystal in the library third period; I owed her an apology. I had a note from Mom crackling softly in my pocket; I'd been severely depressed the whole day, and I'd obviously looked so convincingly sick that Mom almost wouldn't let me go back to school. I'd given the matter some consideration, and decided that if nothing else, I could really use a workout. I had hardly sat down before Jim Frye called over,

"Hey, Johnnie Ray—heard you really cussed out old Brock yesterday." I shrugged a rather noncommittal shrug. It honestly hadn't occurred to me that my scene with Brock would make the papers. But lo and behold, as I got off the bus, another kid I hardly knew called out to me,

"Heard you punched out Brock—way to go!" He walked on before I could tell him I'd never laid a hand on the old guy.

On my way into the choir room, I spotted Todd coming out. I called out his name, but he didn't seem to hear me; I quickened my pace to catch up with him.

"Hey, Todd, wait up." He stopped and turned.

"Johnnie Ray." He tilted his head in greeting. It was easy to see how down the guy was. His face, though drop-dead handsome as usual, looked different, like his features had fallen a bit. His shoulders looked rounded and stooped, and he stood like a tired, beat-up old man instead of the healthy eighteen-year-old stud he was. He even looked shorter. What a difference a day made. Twenty-four little hours. And so on.

"How are you?" I asked, hoping he could somehow deduce that I didn't mean how's it goin'. That I meant the big How Are You.

He just shrugged and said, "I'm all right."

Which I knew he wasn't. I wasn't sure just where to go from there, conversation-wise, so we stood for an uncomfortable couple of beats before I said,

"Has she gone yet?" Meaning Leslie, of course.

"Yeah." He looked up at the sky for a second, and then down at the tops of his boots. "They packed her off so fast I didn't even have a chance to say goodbye to her." Suddenly he looked me dead in the face, his eyes broadcasting pain like a fifty-thousand-watt radio station broadcasts the hits. "I don't fuckin' know where she is. I don't know how long she'll be gone. I'm never even gonna see my baby. And they didn't even let me say g'bye to her." He blinked rapidly several times, and I could tell his eyes were gearing up to cry. He turned quickly around, embarrassed for me to see him. He was wiping at his eyes with the long sleeve of the striped pullover shirt he was wearing.

So what did I expect the guy to do? Turn to me, not exactly his best friend on earth, and spill the whole plate of spaghetti? Fall into my arms and sob so I could have the opportunity to comfort him, I guess. Anyway, he obviously wasn't the kind of guy to look you right between the eyes and say, "Hey man, I'm hurting." Still, I had the strongest desire to touch him. And I don't mean the sort of crotch-level desire I usually had where Todd was concerned. I just wanted to touch his hand, maybe hug him; tell him I was sorry, that I cared. I'd hugged Todd before, in church youth-group meetings, during Sharing of Love when we all go around the room and hug each other and say, "I love you in Jesus." But this was not quite the time and place for that; and besides, I didn't see where this had a whole lot to do with Jesus. I was at a serious loss for what to do.

Finally, I reached up and put my hand on Todd's shoulder, squeezed it just a little and said, "I'm really sorry, Todd." Ever notice how the words *I'm sorry* always seem the lamest when you want them to mean the most? Todd just shrugged again and said "Thanks."

"You know," I said, "I called you Monday night."

"You did?" I'd never called Todd on the telephone before in my life.

"Yeah. Just to say I was sorry about what happened."

"Really?"

"Yeah. There was no answer, though."

Todd finally looked halfway over his shoulder.

"Thanks. I appreciate that. I really do."

"Look," I said, trying to lighten an unlightenable situation, "why don't you come back into the choir room, we'll sing something. 'Love Me Like a Rock' or something."

"Nah," he said, his back still turned to me, shifting his weight from one foot to the other.

"Look, Todd"—I probably should have just let the man go about his business, but somehow I couldn't seem to do it—"I just, if you ever like want to talk, you know, I just want you to know—I just want you to know I'm there, that's all." I immediately felt a little foolish. I mean, who was I all of a sudden, to start playing Sisters of Mercy with Todd Waterson, one of the sexiest guys in school? I wondered if he might laugh at me, but he didn't. He turned around, finally. Put his hand on my shoulder. Sniffed a big wet sniff.

"You know," he said, "you're the first person who's even talked to me since Monday. A couple of assholes have yelled things at me, like 'Way to go, Todd.' But mostly—shit, I just feel like I've got leprosy or something. All these good little Christians we go to church with are suddenly treating me like Mr. Sin. Like most of them weren't doing the same thing me and Leslie were doing. Or trying to do it. Assholes." He squeezed my shoulder again. "You're all right, Johnnie Ray."

And he turned and started off.

"Todd," I called after him, "you sure you don't want to come in the choir room?"

"Nah," he said without turning around. "Maybe tomorrow." He walked a few more steps, then he turned around.

"Hey, did you really slug Brock in the jaw?"

"Of course not," I said.

"Oh, well." He shrugged and headed off toward the library.

Cherie and Efrem were already sitting in the choir room; as I walked in, I could just hear Efrem's voice over the Foleys' four-handed version of "Classical Gas." Whatever he was pontificating about, he dropped it as I approached.

"I trust you've heard about your friend Todd," Efrem said in lieu of greeting. Cherie wordlessly attached herself to my arm.

"Monday night," I said. "Did you see him? He looks like shit."

"He was just here," Efrem said. "He didn't stay long."

"Did you say anything to him?"

"I *never* say anything to him." He had a point. I started to explain to Efrem that this would be the perfect time to scrape up any human kindness he might have put aside for a rainy day, but I let it slide.

"I'm real sorry about the auditions. Needless to say, Mr. Dead End is a major horse's ass of this or any season."

"Well"—I did my patented nonchalant who-gives-a-shit shrug—"Brock's horse's-assdom is neither here nor there at this point, is it?"

"Perhaps not. By the way, you didn't really bloody the old fool's nose, did you?"

"Of course not," I said. "I just yelled at him. Called him everything short of Grand Dragon of the Ku Klux Klan, cried a little, told him to take his play and sit on it; but I swear to you, no blood was shed."

"I thought not, but one can dream, can't one?"

"Then are you going to the auditions at the J.C. tonight?" Cherie uttered her very first words since my arrival, maybe even her first of the day.

"Hark"—Efrem cupped a hand to his ear—"Garbo talks."

"Yes, Mommy," I nuzzled Cherie's sweet-smelling hair, "I think I *will* go to the auditions at the J.C. tonight." I hadn't actually decided for sure that I was going until Cherie asked me. I'd been toying with the concept of actually having a few weeks of evenings free for a change, and it didn't seem such a bad idea. "I've got a few things to take care of before tonight, though. I've got to have a little talk with Brock, for one."

"To apologize?" Efrem asked, horror in his eyes.

"To talk my way out of having to enter the old fart's class for the remainder of the semester, I hope."

"How come?" Cherie said, speaking into my shoulder as usual.

"Because there won't be one helluva lot to do in there for those of us not involved in the show. Because I've already passed the class even if I never go back. Because if I never see Brock's ugly shriv face again, it'll be much, much too soon. Need I go on?"

"Please don't," Efrem said through a snorting little laugh.

The three of us sat and listened to Johnny Foley do "Alice's Restaurant." He knows the whole twenty-some-odd-minute version by heart, and performs it at the drop of a hat. He had gotten to the whole "eight-by-ten color glossy photos under the pile of garbage" part, when Cherie said, even softer than usual: "Can't wait till Saturday." She smiled a satisfied little smile at the mention of our weekend plans. My stomach tightened in advance nervousness at the thought of it. I wondered if maybe I hadn't made a big mistake.

I excused myself from the choir room a few minutes before first period and tromped on over to the Drama bungalow. Brock looked a little bit apprehensive at the sight of me, but he didn't mention our little difference the morning before—no talk of suspension, no nothing—and damned if I was gonna bring the subject up. It was a very easy matter to convince old Brock to let me finish out the semester with a paper, a report on some play or other.

"That'd be fine, Rouss," Brock said, forcing a smile that twitched a little on one side. "Do you have a particular play in mind?"

"No," I lied. "Not yet." Actually, I planned to write a paper about *The Boys in the Band*. I'd read it eight or nine times, had in fact taken it out on indefinite loan from the public library—meaning the librarians didn't exactly know I had it. I had most of the play memorized, in fact, so it would be a cinch to rattle off a report good enough to get by Brock, who thought you were a genius if your subjects and verbs agreed. And the thought of old Brock reading a report on *Boys in the Band* was automatic laughs. The old guy was a homo-hating asshole if there ever was one—he once referred to Tennessee Williams as a pervert, in class.

Anyway, I probably wouldn't have to see Brock more than once or twice for the rest of the semester, and I also wouldn't have to watch the cast of *Hooray for Whatnot* rehearsing constantly during sixth period. Both of which spelled relief as far as I was concerned.

I went to the library third period. Mr. Katz winced a little while giving me permission to skip his class again. But there really wasn't much he could say—I was an Honor Scholar, and besides, we were covering the Thirties in class, and I knew just about everything worth knowing about the Thirties from the movies. Crystal was in the library, at the same table in the same chair I'd found her in on Monday. She smiled as I approached.

"I'm sorry about yesterday," I said.

"That's okay," she said. "I heard about what happened."

"I didn't hit him."

She smiled, rolled her eyes. "I know that." She dug the deck of cards out of her purse and gave them a quick shuffle. "You ready?" she asked.

"I guess."

"There's still an awful lot on your mind," she observed, correctly, "but let's give it a shot, anyway." She placed the deck facedown between us on the table. "Now, just clear your mind as best you can. Don't try to concentrate or anything, just go with your first impulse. Just colors, black or red, that's all."

I shrugged a here-goes-nothing.

I got thirty-seven out of fifty-two.

Crystal looked across the table at me and smiled as if to say, "I told you so."

CHAPTER

7

I ASSUMED THE AUDITIONS WOULD be held in the theater, but when I got there the place was shut up tight as a drum; there was nobody at all around the theater building. It was about five o'clock—most of the day classes were over, and night school wouldn't be starting for a couple of hours. Since our school doesn't have a theater of its own, we always do our plays in the J.C.'s theater, which was the only building on the whole campus I was familiar with. I was beginning to wonder if this was the right day. I felt a little tremble starting in the middle of my stomach; I was starting to feel like a little kid who's lost his Mom somewhere in Disneyland.

"Okay, Johnnie Ray," I said to myself, sotto voce, "you can either start looking for the right room, or you can jump the next bus and go home." I looked past the theater building toward the classrooms, building after building of them—a blind search didn't look all that promising. But instead of just making a decision, any decision, and going with it, I stood there for a while, my arms wrapped halfway around myself, shifting weight from one foot to the other, stuck there in a holding pattern for a few minutes. After a while, the basic chicken-shit in me started rapping, telling me things like, "Hey, it wouldn't be any fun, anyway, and besides, I probably wouldn't even get cast," and I had just about decided to forget the whole thing and go home, when a guy with hair down to his shoulders walked past me.

I called out "Excuse me," but the guy just kept walking. I said "Hey," and started after him. I was pretty sure it wasn't somebody from my school, so I assumed he knew his way around better than I did. He was wearing old faded jeans, and his walk reminded me of Todd's, except this guy was a little wider in the ass than Todd. He wasn't walking all that fast, but he was taller than me and I had to make a real effort to catch up with him. Which I finally did.

"Excuse me," I said again, and the guy finally stopped.

"Yeah?"

"Uh."

Yes, that's what I said. Uh.

"Uh?" The guy sort of half-smiled, and one eyebrow went up. He had thick, dark Tyrone Power eyebrows that looked like they might be planning to merge into one big brow. He seemed to have too many teeth for the size of his mouth, and the teeth were fighting it out for space, doubling up in front of each other in the process. His hair was much longer than I usually like on a guy, parted just off center and tucked behind a big Clark Gable ear on one side.

He was cute.

Really cute. Cute enough to briefly render me a total mongoloid, which is my usual reaction when I'm really attracted to a guy, which I immediately was to this guy.

Funny thing: he wasn't even my type, which is blonds. And he wasn't really handsome; not ridiculous movie-star handsome like Todd. But, I'll tell you, there was something about the guy that really tied my tongue. The guy looked down at me (he was a full head taller) and cocked his head to one side.

"Somethin' I can help you with?" His voice was deep and husky; he'd be a bass if he sang.

"Do you know where the auditions are being held?" I finally managed to spit it out. My voice came out strange, even higher pitched than normal. "For the student projects, I mean."

"Sure do. I'm headed there myself." He started walking and gestured with his head for me to come along.

Walking along the corridor, I found myself constantly gravitating toward the guy. Every now and then my arm would just touch his, and it was like wiping over an electrical outlet with a wet rag. When I got really close to the guy, I could smell him. Not like disgusting unwashed B.O. or anything, just his smell.

"You must be from the high school," he said after a moment.

"Uh-huh."

A few more steps.

"What's your name?"

"Johnnie Ray."

"Like the singer, huh?"

"Yeah." I was surprised. Not that many people close to my age have ever heard of Johnnie Ray, the singer, since most of his hits came out before we were born.

Mr. Long-Hair started singing "Walking My Baby Back Home," way off key and sort of on one note. He was no singer.

"What's your name?" I asked, just for conversation.

"Well now," he said, looking straight ahead, "they often call me Speedo."

Which, of course, is the first line of "Speedo" by the Cadillacs. Which I'm sure he thought I didn't know, so I said, "And I suppose your *real* name is Mr. Earl?"

He stopped dead in his tracks, smiling that funny half-smile again. I'd surprised him—I thought I might.

"Yeah." He put his hands on his hips and just stood there looking at me for a second with his head cocked off to one side again.

"Yeah." He started nodding and smiling, really smiling this time. You know how some people smile with just their lips or just their mouths. Well, this guy smiled with his entire face. I mean he showed a whole smileful of cute crooked white teeth, and his cheeks came out and his eyes crinkled at the corners, and it was a smile and a half. He offered this big, tan hand to me, and after a second's hesitation, I took it. His hand was very soft, but his grip was strong. I like the feel of it. He pumped my hand vigorously, still nodding and smiling.

"Name's Marshall," he said. "Marshall MacNeill. What'd you say your name was?"

"Johnnie Ray," I said, a little disappointed that he'd forgotten my name so quickly. "Rousseau."

"Johnnie Ray Rousseau," he repeated to himself. "Johnnie Ray Rousseau." He nodded an equivocal little nod and said, "All right." And off he walked, this time humming "Speedo."

"Marshall MacNeill," I repeated his name softly to myself.

I followed Marshall MacNeill halfway across the campus to a

classroom with maybe fifteen people in it, and absolutely no furniture. Not a stick. What people there were (and I didn't recognize
any of them) were either standing or leaning or sitting on the floor,
talking among themselves, most of them smoking cigarettes and
either using the chalk trays beneath the one blackboard for an ashtray or just dropping their ashes onto the linoleum, the sight of
which made me cringe. That's one thing I really hate about
smokers: the world is their ashtray.

Marshall stopped me just as we entered the room, reaching
around me and putting his hand on my shoulder, which sent a
tremble through me I would have been surprised if he couldn't
feel.

He called across the room, "Hey, Libby. Look what I found."

A fat woman sitting in a far corner of the room (talking to a
long-haired bearded guy who looked like Jesus in jeans) turned
around, spotted us at the door, and smiled so big she nearly hit the
bearded guy with her cheek.

"Marsh!" she cried like she'd just sighted her long-lost lover
walking up the road to home. She managed herself up from the
floor with what I considered an amazing lack of difficulty for her
size and did a kind of lumbering waddle over to Marshall and me.
She was one of the fattest women I'd ever seen. She was wearing a
humongous red paisley muu-muu sort of a dress and no shoes and
about thirty-seven bracelets on each arm, and she was dragging a
big dirty macramé purse uglier than Crystal's. She looked a lot like
Mama Cass.

"What'd ja bring me, Daddy?" she said, smiling that big, fat
smile of hers and giving me an obvious once-over, then a twice-
over.

"He followed me home," Marshall said, hooking his arm
around my neck; I ended up with my head practically in his armpit. "Can I keep him?" My blood pressure shot up high enough to

break the machine, and I could practically hear my dick revvin' up for a boner.

The fat lady laughed ha-HA up a full octave and quickly down the scale, and said, "Marshall, you crazy-fuck." Which startled me—I'd never heard a woman say fuck before. "Hi, I'm Libby," she said to me. "You here for the auditions?"

"Of course he is," Marshall said. "Don't you think he'd be perfect for the boy?" He grabbed my face with one hand, pushing my cheeks together and making my lips pooch out, and said, "Just look at this face. Have you ever seen a more innocent face in your life?"

Libby slapped at Marshall's arm and said, "Marsh, would you let go of the child's face. What's your name, baby?"

"Johnnie Ray." It was a wonder I could talk at all: Marshall's arm was still around me, his hand sort of dangling off my shoulder, and it was making me crazy. I'd never had a guy, let alone a guy this cute, be so physical with me before, and I was flattered that this good-looking college dude was being so palsie-walsie; but if he didn't stop touching me, I was going to be in big trouble, erection-wise.

"Well, it sure is good to see you," Libby said. "The turnout from the high school has not been what we'd hoped for."

"How many kids have been in?" I looked around the room again; there was nobody there from school.

"Baby, so far you are *it*," Libby said, ever smiling. Her head moved from side to side when she talked. I took an immediate like to this big dame. "Have you ever done any acting before?"

"Sure I've been in—"

"Shit," she said, "I'm desperate. I'll take you if you can read. If you can repeat what you hear, like a parrot. I need a boy." Suddenly, she looked askance at me, as if trying to read my fine print. "How old are you?"

"Eighteen," I said. Which was a lie. I was a full half-year short of eighteen, but something told me eighteen was a much better answer than seventeen-going-on, so I lied.

"Oh, good," Libby said.

"Street-legal," Marshall said.

Street-legal?

"Cut it out, Marsh," said Libby. "Come sit down," she said, gesturing me away from the door and plopping her great bulk down onto the floor. I sat cross-legged across from her, and Marshall sat down next to me.

Libby leaned forward to talk to me. The soles of her plump feet were black with dirt.

"Now, what we're doing here are basically just class projects. Nobody's gonna see 'em except the class and the instructors. Not exactly a major career move for you as an actor. Anyway, what I'm doing is a one-act about prison. It's called *Lockup*, and it's a very realistic depiction of prison life. The situations are rough and the language is rough. Understand?"

"I guess." I don't use a lot of cusswords myself, but it's not as if I'd never heard any.

"Also," Libby continued, "because this is about prison, the subject of homosexuality is involved."

A chill started at my toes, flew up the length of me, and shot out through the top of my head. I wouldn't have been surprised if my hair had stood straight up.

"Does that bother you?" Libby stared me dead in the eyes.

"No," I said, fighting a tremble.

"You sure?"

"Sure," I said, hoping I sounded surer than I felt.

"'Course it don't bother little Johnny Ray." Marshall smiled and raised an eyebrow at me. "Does it?" And from the way he said that, I got the feeling it was a serious question, like he was trying to get me to admit something. And for some reason, I got kind of bold. I just looked Marshall square in the face and said, "Nope. Not a bit."

"Good," Libby said. "Either way, I've got to have your mom or dad sign a waiver that they understand you'll be involved in a play with quote adult subject matter unquote. Think that'll be a problem?"

"No. My parents are cool." Which was a half-lie. Mom and Dad were decidedly uncool about rough language, rough situations, etcetera. But there wouldn't be a problem because I'd just sign Mom's name myself. I used to do so many sick notes and absence notes to get out of P.E., I sign Mom's name better than she does.

"Great." Libby smiled. "Think you want to read for me?"

"Why not?" I shrugged, hoping I looked mature and nonchalant, which was nothing like I felt.

"Now, there are only four characters in this play. I've already cast three of them with some friends of mine. Marshall's one of them." I looked at Marshall, who smiled mischievously in my direction. "All but the boy. Now he's just a kid, and he's been busted for pot and thrown into the klink with a bunch of hardened criminals. That's the part you'd play." She handed me a script, a bunch of ditto sheets stapled together at the upper left corner and folded open to a page somewhere near the middle.

"Okay," Libby said, "this is your first day in jail. You've been busted on a pot rap, and you've been tossed into a cell with a convicted rapist, who has taken the first opportunity to come on like gangbusters, and you're scared. Shitless." Libby smiled at her own speech. "But as Ponch is coming on to you, you find, to your greater fear and confusion, that while he's scaring the living shit out of you, he's also turning you on. Got that?"

"Uh-huh." I must admit I was a bit surprised to find such goings-on at our local J.C. Maybe this town wasn't so tight-assed after all.

"Great. Okay, top of page nine, starting with Ponch, that's Marsh, and Johnnie Ray, you read Billy; Marsh, I want menacing, I want sex, and Johnnie Ray, I want fear, I want scared shitless. As the scene progresses, I want Marshall advancing, Johnnie Ray retreating, and by the end of the scene I want Johnnie Ray backed into a corner and Marsh practically breathing up the kid's nose; and Johnnie Ray, by that time you're so scared you've practically soiled your bloomers, and at the same time you're so turned on you'd have this man's baby. Get it?"

"Got it," I said.

"Good. Let's go, then."

I took a quick glance at page nine, trying to get some idea of the lines—cold readings make me nervous, and this Marshall person wasn't helping—when Libby says,

"Ready. Aaaaaaand . . . go."

And Marshall jumps into a crouch, and his face takes on this wild-eyed expression that I swear had "rapist" scribbled all over it, and he starts reading:

PONCH. This your first time inna joint?

BILLY. Uh-huh. [*My first line—one word, and my voice cracks on it. And believe you me, it isn't acting—this dude is scaring me to death. "Good fear, Johnnie Ray," Libby says.*]

PONCH. Hey, baby, no problem. No problem. Ponch'll take care of you, baby. Ponch'll take care of you real good. [*At which point Marshall puts his hand on my leg and starts stroking it—just a bit of improv. Libby says, "Good business." And naturally, my dick pops up like toast, and with me in that crouched position, it's all revved up with no place to go. Which means Marshall and Libby probably can't tell that I've just popped a raging bone-on, and also means that I am experiencing some serious discomfort.*]

BILLY. Leave me alone! [*I slap wildly at Marshall's hand, and he takes it away.*] Guard!

PONCH. Hey, baby. Hey, beautiful. [*Marshall reaches up and strokes my face. My heart starts pounding until my whole body feels like one big pulse.]* Don't be like that. You gonna need somebody to take care of you in a place like this, pretty young thing like you. Got nobody to take care of you, you get hurt, get hurt real bad. You wouldn't want that, would you?

BILLY. No. *[My voice is all but inaudible. Libby says, "Good, Johnnie Ray."]*

PONCH. Course not. *[Marshall leans forward. I immediately move back. And we slowly start moving, steadily—Marshall forward, me backward, half crouch, half crawl on all threes with the script in one hand.]*

PONCH. Yeah, you be my punk, I'll take care of you. *[Marshall's hand leaves my face and slowly strokes its way down my neck, to my chest.]*

BILLY. Guard! *[A cry of pure animal panic, let me tell you.]*

PONCH. Yeah, take good care of you, my little punk, my sweet little punk. *[Marshall has me backed all the way into a corner by now, and his hand is at my waist.]*

BILLY. Guard!

PONCH That's right, baby, you and me we gonna be jam up and jelly tight.

BILLY. Guard! Guard!! Guard!!!

I screamed those "guards" so loud and with such fervor that everybody in the room stopped talking. Suddenly you could hear the crickets outside the building. Because when Marshall hit the word "tight" in "jam up and jelly tight," he clamped his left hand directly on my crotch. Which was, of course, rock hard and throbbing like a sore.

Marshall looked deep into me with those little brown eyes of his, and smiled a smile that I thought might have been ridicule, or maybe something else, I couldn't tell, when (it seemed like weeks had gone by) Libby said, "Shit-dang, you guys! That was great."

Which was when Marshall finally removed that big, hot hand of his from my groin. Which was when I finally started breathing again. I said "The Lord is my shepherd" to myself faster and with more feeling than I think it's ever been said before or since, and my dick slowly cooperated to the point where it probably wasn't too too obvious that I was about to burst the buttons of my Levi's.

"Well, Johnnie Ray," Libby said, "needless to say, you've got the part if you want it. Please say you want it."

"I—uh—" I was alternating more hot and cold flashes than a roomful of menopausal matrons, I could still feel Marshall's hand on me, and I was hardly at my most articulate.

"'Course he wants it," Marshall said, and he hooked his arm around my shoulders again. I fought the urge to turn and bury my face in his armpit and said okay.

"Awrite." Marshall shook me by the shoulder. I wriggled out from under his arm (another erection was announcing its arrival), and said to Libby, "That's it then?"

"That's it. We'll rehearse Thursday and Friday nights, seven till about ten, starting next week for the next four weeks. That's not a whole lotta time, so you're gonna hafta learn your lines pretty much on yer own. We'll rehearse at my place, I'll give you the address and the form for your Mommy to sign so she knows you're gonna get raped onstage."

"And *I* get to do it," Marshall said through a smile and a slow, insinuating eyebrow-raise. I blushed, albeit invisibly, and my ears sizzled. The thought of getting raped by Marshall MacNeill, on or offstage, really made my toes curl.

"Well, I better go." I started for the door. "I gotta get a bus or it's kind of a long walk."

"You're gonna *walk* home?" By Libby's tone, you'd have thought I was planning to push a peanut all the way home with my nose. "Where do you live?"

"Just off J Street, near Tenth."

"Marsh"—she slapped Marshall on the shoulder with a chubby bracelet-rattling hand—"take the kid home."

"No, that's—"

"Libby, give a guy a chance to volunteer, why doncha. Sure, cutie, I'll take ya home."

"No, thanks, really. I don't mind the walk." Which I really didn't. I was used to walking. I did a lot of it, since I'd only had a driver's license for about a month before I accidentally totaled my father's V-W Beetle and Dad took away my license. Besides which, the thought of being alone in a car with Marshall Mac-Neill gave me a chill that I couldn't entirely chalk up to the cold breeze coming through the wide-open door.

This dude was messing with my mind. I mean, was he gay? Was he just teasing me because he could somehow tell I was gay? Was he hustling me, or was he like this with everybody? And was it my imagination, or did he just call me "cutie?"

"Don't be ridiculous," said Libby. "You will not walk home."

"Yeah, don't be ridiculous," and Marshall, his hand at the small of my back, maneuvered me out the door. I could hear Libby's "See you next Thursday" as we started down the hall.

CHAPTER

8

IT WAS THE UGLIEST CAR I THINK I have ever seen. Even in the uneven light of the parking lot, I could tell this was one filthy beige beast Marshall MacNeill intended to drive me home in. It was shaped rather like a potato bug; I could see the rust freckles all over the body of it, a thousand dark specks in the yellowish lamplight. There was a thick sweater of dirt all over the car. Some thoughtful person, maybe Marshall, had taken a finger and printed WASH ME PLEASE across the back of the vehicle; that same person, or maybe somebody else, had written BOB across the front.

"Door's open," Marshall said, opening the driver's-side door. The passenger door fought me as if locked as I tried to open it. "Just give it a good swift yank," Marshall advised. Which I did, and the door opened with a sound that reminded me of the guitar feedback on "My Generation" by the Who.

There was a pile of debris on the seat that included one, maybe two complete changes of clothing, half a ham-on-rye, a copy of *Another Roadside Attraction* by Tom Robbins, and one mateless rubber-tire-soled sandal somewhat the worse for wear.

"Just throw that shit in the back."

The seat squealed a protest as I settled in and wrestled the door shut (its hinges did another short Pete Townshend imitation). After a brief difference of opinion with the ignition, Marshall started the car's engine, which sounded like it had eaten too much Mexican dinner.

"What sort of car is this?" I asked over the sputtery sounds of the engine.

"It's a Saab. That's his name on the hood there. Bob Saab." He slapped the radio on, and Lou Reed was singing. And we sputtered our way out of the parking lot and onto L Street.

Marshall didn't say anything for what seemed a long while; every now and then he'd sing along with Lou Reed for a few bars, off-key, "Hey, babe, take a walk owna wiiiiild siiiide." The lack of conversation was making me pretty uncomfortable pretty quickly, and I was just about to ask Marshall how he liked the old J.C., or something equally scintillating, when he suddenly said, "You wanna go over to El Taco, get something to eat?"

"No thanks. I'm not hungry." Which wasn't true; I'm almost

always hungry. The fact was that I was broke—I was only carrying bus fare.

"Well, then, would you mind keepin' me some company while I have something to eat?"

"No, I suppose not." I was obviously going to end up getting home later than I'd planned to be, and Mom was sure to have something to say about it. But this Marshall person really had me going: I wasn't sure if I liked him or not, but he sure had me interested in finding out. Besides, he was driving.

El Taco had recently become a favorite hangout for some of the school's less study-oriented students, the sort of people I know only by sight and whom I tend to avoid at all costs. Through the glass front of the building I could see several such people sitting, standing, leaning, and sprawling around, some really redneck-looking guys and a group of black kids from the other side of town, with a wary aisle's distance between the two groups. There was nobody in there I knew or cared to know, and it was a toss-up as to which bunch made me more nervous. I was sincerely glad when Marshall pulled old Bob Saab up to the drive-thru window, ordered quickly, and pulled the car into a parking space way off in a corner, just outside the glow of the tall streetlamps that illuminated the lot.

The spicy food fragrances coming off the greasy white paper bag in Marshall's lap made me drool like one of Pavlov's puppies. I was wondering how I was going to be able to stand it, sitting in this funky little car watching Marshall eat, when Marshall pulled a small white-paper-wrapped bundle out of the bag, and handed it to me (along with six or seven paper napkins).

"What's this?" I accepted the warm white whatsis only reluctantly, holding it rather as if it were ticking.

"It's a chicken taco," he said, unwrapping his own. "You eat them. I believe it is the chicken taco that truly separates Man from the lower primates."

Still I hesitated to open it.

"I'm buying," Marshall said, and took a big, crackly bite.

"Thank you. Very much."

Marshall said "Forget it" through a mouthful of taco.

We just sat and ate for a while, filling the car with crunching and smacking. I was in taste-bud heaven—there are few things in life I enjoy more than a good taco. Marshall handed me the extra-large cherry Coke he'd been slurping, and when I went to lift the plastic lid off the cup, he said, "Use the straw, for chrissakes. I'm not diseased or anything." Actually, I'd been concerned that he might not want a mouthful of *my* cooties.

"So, you're probably a senior, right?"

"Uh-huh."

"Gonna be an actor when you grow up? Movie star?"

"Eventually," I said. I could tell he was making fun of me a little, and it kind of stung.

"Eventually?"

"Yes." I handed him the cherry Coke back. "See, the way I look at it, I really don't want to do the whole, you know, *ac*ting thing. You know, cattle calls and commercials and all that. I mean, there aren't all that many parts for black actors, especially one like me. I'm not a type, or anything. So I figure, if I become a success as a singer first, well then they write vehicles especially for me, see? I'm a singer, basically."

"Basically," Marshall repeated. He turned to me and handed me one of those crooked half-smiles of his and said, "You got it all pretty well figured out, haven't you? For a senior in high school, I mean."

I wasn't sure if he was razzing me or not.

"Well"—I was starting to get just a bit defensive here—"I certainly don't intend to hang around here after graduation."

Marshall smiled all the way. "I see. Going to a major university, are we? U.S.C?"

"U.C.L.A.," I said, a little smug pride leaking out from the corners of my mouth. "I've already been accepted." I have to plead guilty to getting a little bit smug about being accepted to U.C.L.A. I mean, nobody in my family has ever even *been* to college.

"None of this junior college shit for you, huh?"

"No way. Junior college is just high school with ashtrays." That line I picked up from Efrem. Marshall lifted a thick eyebrow at me and I said, real fast, "No offense."

"None taken." Marshall sucked taco sauce off his fingers. He had really nice lips.

"What about you? You an actor?"

"Nah. Not me. I'm only doing this one-act as a favor to Libby. I'm a filmmaker."

"Really? What kind of movies? I *love* movies."

"Not movies." Marshall rolled his eyes like I'd just accused him of making mud pies out of doggie-do. "*Films.*"

"Oh. You mean Art."

"That's right, Sonny. Art. Somethin' wrong with that?"

"No, nothing at all." And that was just about where my interest in Marshall's career goals came to a halt so fast it left tire tracks. As far as I can tell, a movie is something you go see to have a good time, and a Film is something you go see because you somehow got the idea that watching it will make you a Better Human Being or something.

Movies I love. *Film* you can keep.

"So have you made any *Films* yet?"

"One. I'm almost finished with the editing. I'll be showing it soon. That's why I'm here."

"What's why you're here?"

"To make a film," he said in a tone of voice that let me know it was his turn to get just a bit defensive. "And show it. Believe it or not, the film department here is halfway decent. But best of all, it's cheap. Dirt cheap. Not everybody can go to U.C.L.A."

Which made me feel a little cheesy for waving my U.C.L.A. banner all over the place like I was at the Rose Bowl or something.

"Not that I couldn't get accepted," he continued, "but who's got the money?"

"Couldn't your parents—"

"My father ended the dole the second I turned twenty-one. I've been living on my savings since—"

"How old are you?"

"Twenty-four."

"Twenty-*four*?"

"Well, you don't have to say it like that."

"I didn't mean—"

"You'd think I'd just told you I was Methus'lah or something."

"No, it's just that—"

"Chicken—"

"I just thought you were younger than that, that's all!" Which was true. I assumed Marshall was twenty or so—twenty-one, tops. "You just look young, that's all!" I realized I was yelling. "God Bless!"

There was a pause you could slice, dice and julienne with a Veg-O-Matic.

Finally, Marshall said, "God Bless?"

"Leave me alone, huh?"

"I'm sorry." Marshall put his hand (warm and a little sticky from tacos) on mine, as if it were the most natural of acts. "I get real touchy about shit sometimes."

"I didn't mean anything." I couldn't help looking down at Marshall's hand—I guess I couldn't quite believe it was where it was—and he took it away so fast you'd think it had caught fire.

"I know you didn't. I'm sorry." He crunched his taco wrapper and napkins into a ball, stuffed them into the greasy bag, and dropped it all on the floor by his feet, then started the car as fast as it would kick over and peeled out of the parking lot.

He drove in silence for a few minutes. I didn't know what to say, or even if Marshall wanted to talk to me at all, anymore, ever.

"I took a few years off after college," he said suddenly, out of nowhere. "Went to Europe. Lived in Paris for a while. College isn't everything."

"I don't recall saying it was." I hoped we weren't going to fight.

"My father thinks it is."

"What about your mom?"

"She's dead."

"I'm sorry." I thought of life without my mom, and tears sprinted into the corners of my eyes.

"I was real young. I hardly knew her. I was raised by my grandmother, mostly. She's Cherokee. Full-blood."

"Really?"

Marshall nodded once. "She gave me my middle name: Two-Hawks."

"Two-Hawks?"

"It's on my driver's license. Wanna look for yourself?" He reached toward his back pocket.

"No, I believe you." And of course I did. My folks are from the Louisiana bayou country, and out there, people will name their kids just about anything. So there are some pretty unusual names in my family, too. I've got an aunt Beulah Leola and an aunt Toot (rhymes with "foot") and a third cousin who was born the night the Russians launched Sputnik, and whose actual legal name is Sputnik. Unusual names are no big deal for me. It was only that it would never have occurred to me that Marshall MacNeill might be one-quarter Cherokee; mostly, I guess, because he wasn't very dark—although now that he mentioned it, he did have cheekbones clear up to his eyes. And it was such a beautiful name: Two-Hawks.

"You've got some Indian blood in you too, haven't you?"

"Matter of fact, I do." My mother's grandfather was a full-blooded something-or-other. I'm not sure what. I just remember that they often referred to him as the Old Injun. "How could you tell?"

"Your cheekbones. And the slant of your eyes."

Nobody said anything for a moment, and then Marshall said (to himself, I suppose), "They're beautiful people. Native Americans."

I wanted to ask him what it was like to be without your mother, but then I thought: how would he know? So I didn't say anything for a while, and neither did he.

We seemed to be hitting every possible red light. At one of them, Marshall turned to me and said, "Sing something."

"What?"

"You're a singer, right? So sing something."

"Here in the car?"

"No, at Carnegie-fuckin'-Hall," he said, smiling. And I thought, what the hey. I closed my eyes (I usually do when I sing), and the first song that came into my head was "Drift Away." It's one of my favorite songs these days. One of those songs that, when it comes on the radio, I have to stop whatever I'm doing and just listen. And it almost makes me cry, every time I hear it.

I sang "Day after day I'm more confused," then decided the key was too high and downshifted about a third for the next line. When I got to the chorus, I was snapping my fingers in time.

I did the chorus twice, by which point we were stopped at yet another red light. I opened my eyes, half expecting to find Marshall laughing his head off; but he was just looking at me, with an expression I couldn't fathom. And he said, "Wow. You really are a singer."

And I was immediately pleased and proud and embarrassed all

at once, and I looked away out my window and said, "Well, I'm going to be, anyway."

"You already are." Marshall pulled away at the green light. "Why'd you pick that song? That's one of my favorite songs."

"Really? Mine, too."

"Yeah? Why?"

"Why you?"

"I asked you first."

"Well . . ." I hesitated a bit. While I was taking a definite liking to this Marshall MacNeill, I still wasn't any too sure just how much I could trust him, how much I could really tell him about myself. How I felt about things. I went ahead, anyway. "Well, I guess it's because to me, music isn't just something to listen to. It's like . . . it's like an escape. It's like no matter how bad it gets sometimes, the music's always there. And there's almost nothing so bad that music won't make me feel at least a little better. I can almost always just . . . well, get lost in the rock and roll. And drift away. Y'know?"

"Yeah," Marshall said so softly I could barely hear him. "I know."

And I could tell he really did know. He knew exactly what I was trying to say, despite my not saying it all that well. And he felt the same.

I pulled a Chapstick out of my pocket and waxed my lips. Before I could return the tube to my pocket, Marshall held out his hand.

"May I?"

I handed him the little black cylinder and I watched him apply the balm to his lips. It seemed such an intimate act to me, like a kiss almost. It made me shiver a little to watch it. When he handed it back, I couldn't help but touch it quickly to my lips again before snapping on its little cap and shoving it back into my pocket.

"There's another song," Marshall said. "You may not know it—

they only play it on the jazz station. It says about when you're feeling down and out, and don't know what to do, and if you don't get help quick you won't make it through the day . . ."

And then he sang, as much as you could call it singing, "couldja call on Lady Day? Couldja?"

He sort of shrugged and half smiled.

"I'm no singer."

When we got to my house, I didn't much want to get out of the car.

"Well, thanks for the ride. And the taco. And everything."

"Hey, no charge."

"So I guess I'll see you next week."

"Yeah."

"Well, I'll see ya." I held out my hand for Marshall to shake. It's not as if I'm this big hand-shaker as a rule—but, boy, did I ever want to touch him. He took my hand and just held it, with very little in the way of up-and-down motion. And when we finally let go, Marshall seemed as reluctant as I was.

And man, was my heart doing drumrolls. I just managed to gasp "I'll see ya," body-block the car door open (with the sound of wrenching metal), and sort of half tumble out of the car.

I stood on the sidewalk, hands in pockets, and watched Marshall kick Bob into gear and take off down the street. He hit the car horn a rather anemic beep-beep as he turned the corner.

Mom was at the stove making gravy when I walked in.

"Boy, where you been?" She barely looked up from the thick, muddy-looking roux she was stirring so vigorously.

"At the J.C., Ma. I told you this morning. I'll be in my room, okay?"

"Dinner will be ready soon."

"I'm not real hungry, Ma."

"Johnnie Ray Rousseau, have you been snacking between meals? I've told you and *told* you about that."

"I know, Ma. I'm sorry, just wasn't thinking."

"Well, you'd just better *start* thinking, Little Mister. Use that long head for something more than a hat rack," and blah blah blah, I was in my room by then. And I'm sure Mom went right on talking for quite a while. She does that.

I was so full of feelings, I felt like I was a balloon and the birthday boy was blowing me up, and my chest could just burst any second. I felt strangely happy, happier than I could remember ever feeling before; yet a lump grew in my throat, and I felt tears in my eyes. My fingers still felt Marshall's touch, and I found myself repeating Marshall Marshall Marshall like a mantra.

It was one very powerful, extremely confusing collection of feelings. So much so that I found it practically impossible for a long while to do much of anything. I spent the next couple of hours just lying back on my bed. No music on or anything.

I just lay there and just, *felt*.

CHAPTER
9

I DREAMED I WAS STANDING NEXT to Marshall's car, leaning into the open driver's-side window. I looked into his face, and he was smiling, and talking to me quite animatedly. But I couldn't hear him. Like a television with the sound turned off.

And suddenly I had no pants on, and my dick was hard. And Marshall stopped talking and just smiled at me, as if he knew every secret of my soul. As if he'd found my letters, and read each one out loud.

I woke up suddenly, just as the switch clicked clicked clicked behind my balls. And I was shooting into my underpants. Again and again and again.

Todd body-blocked his way into the choir room, backpack and guitar in hand; he looked up to where we sat (meeting my eyes for a moment), and started up the tiers toward us.

"Here he comes," Cherie whispered, as if I hadn't noticed. She'll do that sometimes—just up and state the totally obvious like that—and it makes me smile.

I nudged Efrem in the arm and sing-songed through my teeth, "Now you just make nice to him, or I'll break your ar-rm."

"Okay, okay."

"How's it goin', you guys?" Todd almost smiled. He was playing Act Like Nothing's Wrong, but he wasn't terribly good at it.

Cherie whispered hello halfway into my shoulder, and Efrem managed to say "How's it goin'" without sounding too too sarcastic. And I said, "How are you?" I looked into Todd's eyes and hoped he wouldn't just say "All right" or something. And of course he said, "All right," and went to stow his guitar away.

Halfway through his hook shot I said, "Let's do 'Blackbird,' okay?" One of the things Todd Waterson is proudest of in his whole life is that he can play the entire guitar part to "Blackbird" by heart. It had taken him weeks to teach himself that song—he's not exactly Hendrix, after all. I remember seeing him, lunch hour after lunch hour, folded up into a corner of the choir room (often with Leslie curled up against him), frowning with concentration, the tip of his tongue peeking out of the side of his mouth as he practiced the fingerings over and over.

"'Blackbird'?" He lowered the guitar case to his side.

"Yeah."

"That's her favorite song." Meaning Leslie's, of course. And the look on Todd's face when he said that, well it could nearly make you cry. It was as close to a real smile as he'd probably had on his lips for days, but if I wasn't mistaken, there were tears gathering at the corners of his eyes.

"I know." Why else would a guy knock himself out like that just to learn a song?

"Will you sing it?" Todd clicked open the guitar case and lifted out the shiny instrument.

"Try and stop him," Efrem said.

Todd slid his fingers into the intro and tapped the stiletto-point toe of his boot against the floor, head down, his yellow-gold hair nearly obscuring his face. I closed my eyes and sang, "Blackbird singing in the dead of night/Take these broken wings and learn to fly. . . ."

Todd did the accompaniment without a single hitch, and when we finished there was some applause. And I felt so good, so warm, a feeling like Saturday morning in bed and pancakes for breakfast.

"Nice job," I said, and opened my eyes, feeling so good I dared to touch Todd, softly, on the knee.

"Thanks." He looked up from his guitar, and he was smiling his perfect smile. And his eyes were shiny with tears. I looked into Todd's pale-blue eyes, and it occurred to me for (strangely) the very first time that Todd must love Leslie. Really love her. He was wearing his love for Leslie Crandall (and his hurt at having lost her, he knew not for how long) like a gaudy floral-print necktie. You could see it for blocks.

And I could only assume that Leslie loved Todd as well. After all, these two didn't just suck face on the senior lawn (though heaven knows they did that, too); they made love. Probably on as close to a regular basis as they could manage. And now Leslie was carrying Todd's baby inside her. And all at once, I was jealous. Jealous of Todd, of the love he felt for Leslie, jealous of hers for him, even jealous of his pain. And of course I immediately felt like shit for feeling jealous.

It was nothing new. Just the same old I Want a Boyfriend Blues I'd been having in one form or another since I was twelve years old. Only stronger, more urgent now than ever before. Because I was seventeen and it was spring. Because there were Todd and Skipper and entire locker rooms full of sexy guys, seemingly put on the earth for the sole purpose of making me crazy, and there's only so much unrequited lust anybody can take. But mostly because of Marshall.

I had Marshall MacNeill on the brain.

I'd thought about him almost constantly since I'd left his old piece-of-shit Saab the evening before. I'd had that dream about him just before waking up in the morning and then beat off thinking about him before leaving for school. On the bus, while pretending to review irregular French verbs, I reviewed everything I could remember about Marshall, his every look and word and movement of dark, thick eyebrow from the first time I laid eyes on him walking past me down the hall at the J.C. There were two shiny little images of Marshall MacNeill in Todd Waterson's eyes before he blinked them back (along with some tears), gave his hair a flip, and reached down to repack his guitar.

Todd stowed his guitar on top of the cabinet, sniffed a wet sniff, and said "See you, guys." I said "See ya, Todd," and he left. Cherie was attached to my right arm, and Efrem was talking and talking about something or other, and I was thinking about what it might feel like to kiss Marshall's lips. The thought of it made my lips itch and started my dick to getting hard, and I tried to think about something else (anything else); but it was like trying not to think about pink elephants. So I thought the Twenty-third Psalm to myself, and I guess some of the words must have leaked out of my mind and out of my mouth, because Cherie said "What?" And

Efrem gave me a look and said, "You haven't heard a word I've said."

And I had to admit I hadn't. And Efrem said, "What's on your mind, Clem?" And I wanted to, God how I wanted to tell him! It would have poured out of my mouth like Kool-Aid from a pitcher: "His name is Marshall Two-Hawks MacNeill and his eyebrows and his ears and O-my-God his smile and he's part Cherokee and I think he likes me and God Bless America, I think he's even gay!"

I didn't say that, of course. I just said, "Nothing." Efrem didn't believe me, of course. Neither did Cherie. Who would?

And I really did think so. Think Marshall was gay, I mean. I'd decided that on the bus, after thinking over everything Marshall had said and done. I was practically sure. And the thought that Marshall MacNeill might indeed be gay made him suddenly more exciting, more desirable to me than Todd or even Skipper, both of whom I knew beyond a shadow of a doubt were straight.

I had Marshall MacNeill like a new strain of flu for the rest of that Thursday and most of Friday. I wrote his name over and over, in every conceivable calligraphy, on the inside flaps of the brown-paper slipcovers on my school books. Mr. Katz caught me daydreaming about Marshall's arm around me, and the wonderful funk of his armpit; and when I couldn't remember what WPA stood for, Katz turned up his lip and gave me a look, and I knew it would be a cold day in you-know-where before he'd be letting me out of his class again, Honor Scholar or no. In the gym, I worked out with new purpose, with the thought that the better I could make myself look, the better my chances that Marshall MacNeill might want me.

I wondered how I would survive an entire week before seeing him again.

I was, in fact, so completely preoccupied with Marshall that on Friday during lunch, when Cherie said, "You haven't forgotten about tomorrow, have you?" I had indeed forgotten. It was a rude splashdown back into immediate reality. And my immediate reality was that I had a date to make love (or at least attempt to make love) with Cherie Baker on Saturday afternoon.

I got that uncomfortable gas feeling in my stomach.

CHAPTER
10

I STILL HAD IT SATURDAY MORN-
ing. I'd hardly slept all night, and I couldn't remember any dreams. It wasn't a particularly cold morning, but I trembled like it was ten below. My stomach felt as if I'd swallowed a brass bookend; I stared down a plate of grits and eggs until I couldn't stare anymore, then I gave up and excused myself from the table. Mom said, "What's the matter, baby? Don't you feel well?" I said, "I'm okay, Ma," and headed off to my room.

I lay on my bed with my eyes closed and played *Goodbye Yellow Brick Road*, all four sides all the way through, twice, trembling and trying not to get the dry heaves. By which time it was nearly noon, which was when I was supposed to meet Cherie at her house. I was still trembling, so I put a jacket on even though it wasn't cold.

Mom was bent over the old Singer Touch-N-Sew, zigzag-stitching a hem on a dress.

I called, "I'm going to Cherie's, Ma," over the sound of the sewing machine.

"Don't make a nuisance out of yourself," Mom said, never taking her eyes off her stitch.

"I won't, Ma." One of the biggest fears of Mom's life is the thought that a child of hers should visit someone's house long enough to become a nuisance. I nearly told her Mr. and Mrs. Baker weren't home, but thought better of it.

Dad was out in the front yard, crouched over a sprinkler head, trimming the grass around it with a pair of shears. He had on a pair of old work pants and a tank-top undershirt. It is without fear of contradiction that I can say that I've got the sexiest father of anybody I know. Most of the men in town Dad's age are fat and bald and wear polyster leisure suits. My dad looks like Harry Belafonte. I mean it: everybody says so. In fact, now and then some total stranger will stop Dad on the street and beg for an autograph. He was on the boxing team in the army, and he's still built like a boxer—arms like a weightlifter, even though he's hardly lifted anything heavier than a forkful of food since the Korean War. What with Mom, who looks like Dorothy Dandridge, especially when she gets all dolled up, I often wonder how I could spring from two such good-looking people and end up looking so, well, commonplace.

I could never tell him, of course, but I must admit to having sort of a crush on my dad. I mean, he's so strong and so very handsome. When I was a kid, up until I was about thirteen, Dad used to wake me up on Saturday mornings by lying full-out on top of me and bouncing the bed. Then he'd rub his rough face against mine and say, "Wake up, Bonie." That was his name for me when I was a kid: Bonie Maronie—because I was so skinny, I guess. He'd always have that just-out-of-bed warmth to him, and sort of a funky, sour morning smell that for some reason I liked. That was one of the best things in my whole life, those Saturday morning wake-up calls. He up and stopped doing it all of a sudden when I turned thirteen, about the same time he decided I was too old to sit in his big recliner chair with him and cuddle.

I miss it.

Anyway, I stood just outside the front door and watched the muscles in Dad's big back moving underneath his shirt for a minute before starting out for Cherie's. I called "See ya later, Dad."

"Going to see Cherie?"

"Yeah."

Dad smiled his handsome "Day-o" smile that probably gives some of our little town's Mormon white ladies some real problems. He gave me a look, a sort of man-to-man conspiratorial look (or so it seemed to me), and said, "You got everything?"

"Uh-huh."

By "everything," Dad was asking if I had a rubber with me. I swear. A couple of months before, Dad took me aside just as I was on my way to Cherie's. He led me over to the far side of the garage, and put his arm around me and said, "You're seeing a lot of this girl."

"Uh-huh."

"Now I know I don't have to go into a whole speech about the birds and bees. I'm sure you know about all that."

I said "Uh-huh." But the fact is I didn't know diddly.

"You protecting yourself, I hope."

"Protecting myself?" What *was* the man talking about?

"Of course, son. I'm sure you think very highly of this girl, but I'm sure you don't plan to marry her right away. At least I hope not."

Which was when it finally dawned on me that he thought I was screwing Cherie. Actually, I was teaching her macramé.

"Dad," I said, "you really don't have to worry about that."

"She said she's taking care of it," he said with a knowing look. "Didn't she? They'll say that, young girls will." He looked around in a quick B-movie is-the-coast-clear look, then pulled the little square foil packet out of his back pocket. "Protect yourself, son. Always." And he pressed the little packet firmly into my palm. Then he squeezed my shoulder and gave me a little wink and said "Be good." It didn't seem like the time to explain to him that I was not putting it to Cherie Baker or any other girl, nor did I have the slightest desire to do so. So I tucked the rubber into my back pocket and said "Thanks, Dad," trying to look as nonchalant as possible, and started off.

"Oh, and son—" Dad gestured me back. "Top drawer of the nightstan' on my side. When you need more."

So here I was, ready to actually do it with Cherie for the first time, with Dad assuming I'd been doing it for months—I'd gotten into the habit of carrying a rubber around in my wallet, and taking a new one out of the folks' bedroom every so often, throwing away the old one. From the smile on Dad's face, it was obvious he had no idea that if I had eaten any breakfast, I'd probably be upchucking all over the front lawn.

"You have a nice time, son." Dad waved a dirty-work-gloved hand at me.

"Thanks, Dad."

Cherie lives just a few blocks away, and I seemed to get to her house much too fast. I rang the doorbell, half hoping it wouldn't work, half hoping Cherie's folks had carted her off to Saugus no matter how sick she claimed to be. But she was at the door so fast she must have been standing right at it, doorknob in hand. She was wearing a white halter top that made her breasts look like a tourist attraction, and a pair of faded bell-bottomed jeans. She looked blissfully calm. She whispered "Hi," smiling that smile of hers, and took my hand.

I was having trouble walking. I was having trouble breathing. I looked down at my chest and could see my heartbeat.

"Excuse the mess," Cherie said. This was no hostess cliché, mind you. The house was a mess. It was always a mess. Cherie's mother possesses housekeeping skills comparable to Cherie's English skills. The Bakers have two huge Labradors, and Mrs. Baker chain-smokes Camels unfiltered, so the house perpetually reeks of dogs and cigarettes.

"Can I get you anything?" Cherie asked.

"Uh-uh." In my nervous agitation, I began emptying small overflowing ashtrays into larger ones.

"Please don't do that," Cherie said.

"I'm sorry." I put the ashtrays down and brushed my hands against my jeans. Then stood there, swinging my arms and feeling awkward for what felt like weeks, before Cherie said, "Sure I can't get you anything? A coke. Iced tea. A beer, maybe."

"A beer?" I'd never tasted beer in my life. Oh, I'd been offered it, at cast parties and such, but I've always feared that if I came home with any alcohol in my bloodstream, Mom would somehow know, and go off like a smoke alarm.

"Yeah, a beer. Might calm you down."

I considered it. Maybe a beer. And then I thought, a hypodermic full of rhinoceros tranquilizer wouldn't calm me down.

"No. Thanks. Nothing for me."

"Then maybe we should just go on to bed."

She took my hand again and led me to her room (by far the cleanest place in the entire house) and plopped down on the Grandma-made-it quilt covering her small unmade bed. As I slowly sat next to her, my only thought was: Oh God, what if I don't get hard?

Cherie, wisely not waiting for me to make the first move, leaned toward me, placed one little hand on my chest, and kissed my lips. I'd never really kissed anyone before, so the sensation was brand new. Cherie's lips were very soft, maybe even too soft. I wasn't sure I liked the feeling, but when her little pink tongue wiggled its way between my lips, my dick shot up.

We fell backward into the bed and kissed and kissed. Our tongues introduced themselves and did a wet waltz around our teeth. I had often wondered what another person's mouth might taste like. Cherie's sort of tasted like nothing, which was fine by me. She stroked me up and down my body with her tiny hands, and, taking it as my cue, I began stroking Cherie's back, her hips, her arms. Her body was like her lips. Soft. Soft-soft, as if she were made of meringue. Still, it wasn't unpleasant exactly, and all in all I was surprised just how much I liked it, the kissing part, I mean. Cherie seemed to me to be quite good at it. I briefly wondered who'd taught her how. At one point I must have kissed her too hard, because she suddenly pulled away and said, "Hey, not so rough."

She pulled off her halter top (something I'm sure I was supposed to do), and I touched her breasts with some curiosity, but not much else, while we kissed some more. I didn't much like the way they hung. Her nipples were as big around as tollhouse cookies. They just seemed—I don't know—extreme. After a bit more kissing, which was beginning to lose its novelty, Cherie reached down and began stroking my hard-on through my pants. She looked up at me with a look that I could have sworn was victory. She had probably been none too sure herself if I was going to get hard or not.

"Why don't we get under the covers," she said.

Cherie's naked body was more softnesses, more baby-sweet scents. She lay on her back, and her breasts seemed to want to fall into her armpits. She almost hoisted me on top of her, and she took my penis into her hand. Her little hand couldn't quite encircle it. She had just begun guiding it into her when I remembered my friend the rubber.

"Um, shouldn't I, y'know, use, something?"

"Unh-uh: I'm on the pill," she whispered.

And I thought, Wow. The Pill.

And it suddenly occurred to me, for the very first time (if you can believe it), that Cherie had obviously done this before. Probably often. I was just beginning to fret about whether or not I might measure up to however many guys she might have been with before in her life, when all of a sudden Cherie lifted and I sort of fell, and I was inside her.

I caught my breath. A long tremble started at my head and sprinted down my back. The feeling was all but indescribable. Warm and wet and nearly unbearably delicious. It felt so good I giggled. It felt so good I bit my lower lip. It felt so good I was hardly all the way inside her before I came, crying out as if someone had jumped out from behind a door and yelled Boo!

"I'm sorry," I said through some ragged breaths.

"It's all right." Cherie stroked my back. "Just wait a minute or two."

And in just a minute or two, we were doing it again. I'd never gotten soft, and when Cherie began to move, I moved with her, almost as if she were teaching me to dance, and almost before I knew it I had the basic step down and we were moving together.

It wasn't a very long time before I could feel another climax slowly sliding the length of me, and I moved faster. Cherie grabbed my behind with her hands and pulled me up and into her with an amazing amount of force. I closed my eyes, and I could just see Marshall MacNeill's face in the red-and-black behind my eyes as I came again. I could hear Cherie making a succession of little kitty-cat noises beneath me before my arms gave way and I collapsed, barely retaining enough presence of mind to fall to one side rather than directly onto Cherie. We both gasped audibly at the sensation of my slipping so quickly out of her wet pussy.

I lay on my back, trembling and short of breath, staring at the ugly old light fixture over Cherie's bed, wondering at the way Marshall MacNeill had popped into my head while I was trying to screw Cherie. I felt a little guilty, as if I had cheated on her or something. Cherie tucked herself into my armpit and stroked my chest. My entire body was exposed nerve endings, and I nearly jumped to the ceiling at her touch.

"Well?" she said after a while.

"Well what?"

"Was it good?"

"Yes. I liked it. I really did."

"And . . ." She seemed to be groping for words to express a difficult thought. "How do you feel?"

"I feel good."

"You know what I mean." She poked at my belly, tickling me. "Do you feel . . . you know, different?"

Then it hit me. She wanted to know if she'd cured me or something. I'd actually managed to forget that that was the whole point of our going to bed together in the first place.

"I don't think so."

"Oh." She drew away from me quickly, rolling as far to the other side of the bed as possible. Which wasn't far—it was only a single bed.

"I'm sorry, Cherie." I touched her shoulder, made a little stroking motion with my hand. "I told you it wouldn't work."

"I know," she said through a sniff, and I knew she was crying. I reached out to hug her, but she drew away, nearly falling off the bed.

"Would you please go."

"Cherie—what can I do?"

"Nothing. It's not your fault, okay? Would you just please go. Would you just do that for me, please?"

"I'm real sorry, Cherie." I slid out of bed and broke speed records getting dressed. Cherie didn't say a word, just sniffed now and then. "Cherie"—I paused at her bedroom door—"you know I love you. As best I can."

"I know." I could just barely hear her.

I went home, feeling lower than the gutters, and managed to get all the way to my room without being seen. I started to put Joni on the stereo, but I wasn't in the mood for any music at all, or even for the French numbers lady. I wrapped myself around a pillow, curled up on my bed, and just lay there, feeling bad. I wasn't even sure if I was feeling bad for Cherie or feeling bad for me or *(e)* all of the above. But I figured I was going to feel pretty much like shit for quite a while.

CHAPTER

11

THE NEXT DAY WAS, OF COURSE, Sunday. And Sunday, of course, meant church. We go every Sunday, Mom and Dad and me, except on the rare occasion when Dad just can't seem to drag himself out of bed in time, or when I for whatever reason just stay home and have cinnamon toast and hot chocolate for breakfast, and watch "Bullwinkle."

I'm not what you'd call terribly religious. Not anymore, anyway. I went through a period when I *was* terribly religious, when I was about twelve years old. It started right after I saw *The Song of Bernadette* on TV. I'd read about it, and I knew Jennifer Jones had won the Oscar for it, and that was my main interest in the movie, initially. As you may or may not know, *The Song of Bernadette* is about Saint Bernadette of Lourdes, who was a poor, ignorant, but basically good French peasant girl back in the late 1800s, who sees a heavenly vision of the Virgin Mary in the village garbage dump. I swear. And she performs several miracles and digs a miraculous healing spring that people still flock to by the thousands, and becomes a nun, and later, a saint.

Well, this was all pretty fascinating to little me, especially since by this time I already had something of a nun fixation. I had seen *The Sound of Music* about thirty-seven times. I loved the Flying Nun. And the Singing Nun (both the real one and Debbie Reynolds in the movie). I knew all the words to "Dominique" by heart, in French. I'm not sure what it was about them, but I did have this thing about nuns. Nothing against the church I was raised in, you understand, but you have to admit the Baptist church is mighty low in the nun department. No nuns or priests or monks; they don't make an awful lot of the Virgin Mary, except maybe at Christmas (after all, where would Christmas be without her?); and you're not likely to hear a lot of talk about heavenly visions of anybody, in or out of garbage dumps.

Anyway, by Bernadette's big death scene, all backlit and with an off-screen chorus singing high, sustained chords all over the soundtrack, I knew I wanted to become a Catholic. Maybe even a priest. Being ineligible for nunhood, it was the best I could hope for.

I went to the public library and crash-coursed the Catholic Church. I learned the Rosary and began reciting it at least once a day while pantomiming the fingering of beads. I spent two weeks' allowance on a large crucifix of indeterminate alloy, and carried it surreptitiously in my back pocket until one day Mom found it making a racket in the clothes dryer.

Needless to say, Mom and Dad were having none of this Catholic business. Mom made it clear that no son of hers was converting to Catholicism while there was a breath left in her body; that Catholics worshipped Mary and prayed to saints and probably weren't going to Heaven; and that I watched too much TV. Any time I come up with a notion Mom finds the least bit out of the ordinary, she rolls her eyes toward Heaven (that great Southern Baptist Convention in the sky) and says I watch too much TV.

Dad asked, "Why would you want to be Cath'lic, son?"

I replied, in my best Jennifer Jones, "Because I wish to dedicate my life to God."

"Well you can just dedicate your life to God in the *true* church, Little Mister," Mom said, giving me the old finger-wag. And I said, "Yes, Mother," but secretly resolved to pray to Saint Bernadette on Mom and Dad's behalf.

This went on for three or four weeks, as I recall. Then a gorgeous blond kid named Mike Mulvaney transferred into my school from Texarkana, Texas, and before long my head was so full of Mike's robin's-egg-blue eyes and Texas accent that there was no room for the Catholic Church, Bernadette of Lourdes, or even Jennifer Jones. Which I can only imagine is all for the best. I really don't see me as much of a priest.

Anyway, since my Catholic period I've done quite a bit of reading about different religions, even tried a couple more on for size. I've read the Bible (cover to cover, like a novel—it lags in spots, but pretty good reading overall), the Book of Mormon (pretty easy to get around these parts), and a good bit of the Bhagavad-Gita (which is truly strange). I seriously considered becoming a Jehovah's Witness for about a week or so. Then Mom found a stack of "Watchtowers" in my room and nearly had a coronary.

Lately, though, I've pretty much given up on organized religion altogether. As far as I can see, nobody's got The Truth, The Answer, or The God. No particular church, I mean. They're all just whistling in the dark, more or less, all of them saying pretty much the same thing over and over with different accents and a name change here and there; not one of them with any more claim to a direct hotline to the Ancient of Days than any of the rest; none of them one baby-step closer to or further away from the Great I Am than, well, I am.

Which is why I've sometimes been heard to say that I don't believe in God. Which is not exactly true, even though I will say it sometimes, for the shock value mostly. What I really don't believe in is church—anybody's church, as I've said. And I also don't buy the Christian Church's God, the frowning old fart in the long white caftan and the long white beard. One hand full of thou-shalt-nots and the other one full of terrible swift sword. Nope—I don't buy it. Not anymore.

Or Mom's God, Dr. Jesus—he's never lost a case. Except he has lost them. Case after case after case. Or the God a lot of the holyholyholy types over at the Baptist church have bought into: Santa Claus, the Tooth Fairy, and the Easter Bunny all rolled into one, with a crown of thorns, yet. Pray for what you want, and—poof!—it's yours. I actually know people who pray for an empty space in a crowded parking lot, and then if someone happens to vacate a space, they'll shout "Praise the Lord," as if they'd just seen water turned to wine, and then tell everybody about it, come the next youth-group meeting.

As far as I'm concerned, there has to be a God, or a god, a creative force of some sort. I mean, all of this could not have just *happened*. A red rosebud, or a skyful of stars, or a Skipper Harris—these are not accidents. On the other hand, I just can't make myself believe any more in a God who actually has time to grant people's wishes, like some fairy godmother in the sky—and plays favorites about it, yet. I mean, one mother will pray that her child not die of leukemia and God says okay; then another one prays the same and her child dies, and this is God? I don't think so.

I figure God (or whoever) made the universe and the world and the whole shebang, left it all in the rather shaky hands of man-kind, and then retired to a nice trailer park in Boca Raton. Every-thing after that, I think—war and peace and hunger and plenty and good and bad and mediocre—can be attributed to and/or blamed on human beings and/or plain old blind luck. Period. End of Sermonette.

Anyway, it was the Sunday after Leslie Crandall was spirited out of town, and in church both Leslie and Todd were quite conspic-uous by their absence. It was Youth Choir Sunday, and the Leslie-

and-Todd Scandal was the talk of the robe room, to the tune of many of the same kids who hadn't spoken to Todd Waterson in days suddenly deciding we all must pray for him and Leslie, because this is what happens when we succumb to sin and blah blah blah. And I'm getting sick to my stomach, because I know for a fact that the only thing keeping a lot of these people from being in the same boat as Leslie and Todd is dumb luck.

It's this kind of thing that makes me wonder why I bother with church at all. Why I do is partly because I like singing in the choir, but mostly because there are some really beautiful guys in youth group—Todd, Mitch Franklin, and a few others—and I usually don't mind enduring a little hypocrisy for the chance to give a guy a hug and tell him I love him (in Jesus, of course), or hold his big sweaty hand during prayer. Before Marshall came along, it was about the best I could do.

From the choir stand, I could see that there were an unusual number of absentees in the congregation. Efrem and I exchanged glances from across the room where he sat with his mom and dad right next to my mom and dad, all four of the parents looking rather as if there were a vaguely unpleasant odor permeating the church. I could also see that Pastor Crandall was about as tense as I'd ever seen him. I could swear I could see the Pastor's back muscles knotting beneath the jacket of his powder-blue leisure suit— Efrem always says Pastor Crandall dresses like a used-car salesman—but maybe it was just the feeling I got watching him attempt to get through his sermon, all the while knowing what his congregation really wanted was an explanation of how he allowed his only daughter to get royally knocked up without the benefit of a proper church wedding. It was so uncomfortable that I had to look away.

My mind wandered, first to Cherie—I wondered how she'd behave the next day, wondered how I should behave. Then to Marshall, remembering his arm around my shoulders, his hand on mine. I started getting hard, and I bowed my head and whispered a quick "Lord is my shepherd" to myself.

CHAPTER

12

AS IT TURNED OUT, IT WAS A waste of energy worrying about Cherie. Come Monday morning, she annexed herself to my right arm as usual, as if nothing had happened, nothing had changed. Which made me a little nervous at first. It was like some two-bit Tarzan movie where one explorer says to another one, "It's quiet—*too* quiet." I tried to hold up my half of a conversation with Efrem while waiting for the other shoe to drop, when Cherie said, "I've been thinking."

"Oh?"

"Why don't you and Todd do 'Blackbird' for the Spring Recital. As an interlude number, I mean."

Which was not the worst of ideas. After all, "Blackbird" was one of my favorite songs, and, modesty aside, I did a pretty fair job of it. Besides which, it was a good opportunity to help Todd feel— well, included, y'know? Frankly, he'd been so awfully tight with Leslie for so awfully long that I'm not sure if he had many friends worth the title, other than her.

When Todd arrived, I flagged him over and he hurried (as much as Todd ever hurries).

"How's it goin'," he said.

"Missed you in church yesterday," I said.

"Yeah," Efrem said, making what was for him a valiant attempt at being pleasant.

"I wasn't feeling well." Todd inspected the toes of his boots.

"Better now?"

"Pretty much."

"Good. You know, we were just talking about you. And I was thinking"—Cherie pinched me on the arm—"that is, Cherie suggested that perhaps we—you and I, that is . . . that we could maybe do 'Blackbird' for the Spring Recital. What do you think?"

"Well . . ."

"It's a real good song for me, and you do the accompaniment so well." I wasn't about to take no for an answer.

"But I'm not even in choir."

"I don't think Mr. Elmgreen will have any problem with that. Do you, Cherie?"

"Of course not."

"Of course not. Well? Would you do that for me? Please?"

"Okay. Sure." Todd smiled, really smiled, treating me to a nice shot of his dimples. He's got one on each cheek, and believe me, boys and girls, a guy could fall into them.

"Great. Mr. Elmgreen's gonna use this Friday's rehearsal as sort of an audition time for the interludes? Can you make it?"

"Sure. I just got study hall fourth period."

"Then it's a deal. In fact, why don't we run through it now."

"Do we have time?"

"Sure."

Todd unpacked his Ovation, gave her a quick tuning, and we did the song. When we were done, Todd had that look on, and I knew he was thinking about Leslie.

"Any word from her?"

"No."

"You'll hear. Soon." A flimsy excuse for a pep talk, but it was the best I could do. Cherie leaned forward and, without letting go of my arm with her left hand, reached out with her right and stroked Todd's hair just one long, slow stroke, letting her hand rest softly against Todd's head for a short moment. And we were all very quiet for a minute, the four of us.

Finally, I said, "So Todd, when do you suppose you'll get around to giving me my ring?" One more lame attempt at levity, I guess.

Todd didn't smile. I think he tried to, but it wouldn't come. He just sort of cocked his head to one side and said, "Guess you'll have to wait till I'm croaked."

And we all laughed.

CHAPTER

13

THE NEXT FEW DAYS ARE LITTLE more than a blur. I was just marking time, impatiently marking time until Thursday, when I'd see Marshall again. I wandered through my classes like a sleepwalker, all but unable to pass myself off as a functioning student. I wrote Marshall's name so many times I had to change all my book covers. I looked him up in the phone book, scribbled down his number, memorized it, and nearly called it about seven thousand separate times. Each time I picked up the phone, my hand shook and my stomach tightened like a crescent wrench, and I'd drop the phone back down without so much as punching one button. And I'd tell myself: He's not home. He won't answer. And besides, even if he were home and did answer, what would I say? Hey there, I realize we've only just met and we're not exactly friends or anything, but I just called to tell you I haven't thought about anything but you for five or six days running.

Sure.

When I actually found myself drawing a big valentine heart around "J.R.R. + M.M.," I told myself as sternly as I could that this had to stop. He's not that cute, I said to myself. He's six years older than you are, I said. And he probably just thinks you're a kid, just some dumb kid. Which, as a matter of fact, you are. Besides, what makes you think he's even gay? Maybe he's just friendly. And even if he is, he's probably got a boyfriend, and even if he hasn't, what in the world would he want with you?

Gave myself a good talking-to. Almost made myself believe it. Almost. None of which helped me get to Thursday as anything less than a certifiable nut-case. How I got through the school day at all is anybody's guess. I couldn't eat a bite of my dinner (I was beginning to worry that all this involuntary fasting might make me lose weight—the very last thing I needed). I was so hyper, I decided to walk to Libby's, even though it wasn't a short walk.

Libby lived east of us, off Avenue C—not the best part of town, but not the worst. I was over three-quarters of the way there (and making record time), when I heard a weak little beep-beep (like the Road Runner with sickle-cell anemia), and I turned to see Marshall's dirty old Saab (a week older and a week dirtier) pulling up beside me. Marshall shoved the passenger door open and said, "Hop in."

I plopped down into that dirty old car seat, and, man, I couldn't have stopped smiling if you'd threatened my life. It felt so good just sitting next to Marshall in that car, I could scarcely believe it.

And Marshall says, "So how's it goin'?"

"All right."

"Good," he said, and his head bobbed absently up and down a few times.

And that was all for conversation for a minute or two, until
Marshall said, "It's good to see you."

"It's good to see you, too."

Another good-sized pause.

"I missed you," he said.

"What?"

"Nothing."

"No, really—what?"

"I said I missed you, that's all. I missed you."

He looked at me quickly, as if to say, Wanna make somethin' of
it?

"I know," I said then. "I mean: Me, too."

I thought I might burst and splatter all over the interior of
Marshall's car. He missed me, too. And he told me so. The idea
that Marshall liked me, the way I liked him, was almost too much
for me to handle right there in a moving vehicle. I was smiling so
hard my face ached; Marshall was smiling too, just driving along
and smiling; and we must have looked like a couple of total
mongoloids, but I didn't care.

Marshall slapped the radio on; Bobby Darin was singing "Mack
the Knife." Marshall started humming along in that no-real-pitch
way he had, and out of nowhere I decided I was going to touch
Marshall, put my hand on his knee or something. I wanted to—
God, how I wanted to—and by golly, I was going to do it. Just
thinking about this made my heart pound louder than anything on
the radio. Made my whole chest pound, in fact, and my head
throb, and my ears ring, and my face go hot. And my dick start to
get hard.

I spent the most part of "Mack the Knife" just getting up the
nerve to put my hand on Marshall, and deciding just what to
touch. Whether to nonchalantly place my hand on his leg, or try
to maneuver my arm around him, or what. We stopped at a red
light, and Marshall's right hand was on the car seat between us,

his fingers tapping rhythm against the ratty upholstery. Bobby Darin was gearing up to the big finish, and I made my move.

I dropped my hand down on the car seat as close to Marshall's as I could get it without actually making skin contact; my head pounding to the point where I could barely hear Bobby at all. I took a couple of deep breaths, trembling so hard I was sure I must be shaking the car, and as Bobby sang "Look out, ol' Mackie's back!" my palm made contact with the back of Marshall's hand.

My heart stopped. I held my breath. Suddenly, I couldn't hear the radio at all anymore. Or the car, or anything else. It was as if the entire rest of the world just clicked off, like television, and everything was white silence; and all I could feel was my hand on top of Marshall's. And in the space of a second, I imagined Marshall turning on me, shaking off my hand, snarling at me and calling me faggot, throwing me out of his car. I shuddered.

And then, Marshall's hand moved. Slowly turned over, so our palms touched, sweaty and hot against each other. And our fingers intertwined. I began to breathe again: big, noisy, chest-heaving breaths. I closed my eyes, not even daring to look down at our hands, and I held Marshall's hand so tightly my fingers hurt. We just sat there for I really don't know how long, just holding hands, me with my eyes shut so tight that tears came, when there was a loud car-horn honk behind us and a man's voice yelled, "Hey, man—it ain't gonna get any greener!"

We quickly unclasped our hands, I opened my eyes, and Marshall shoved Bob Saab into gear. We didn't say anything. I looked at Marshall, his big hands on the steering wheel, his lips, his hair. I knew he had to be the most beautiful man on earth. I felt like singing, but I didn't know any songs good enough for how I felt (Marvin Gaye was singing "Let's Get It On," which was real close, but not quite). I felt like tap-dancing up and down the sidewalk, and I don't even know how to tap-dance. So I just looked.

Neither of us said another word before we got to Libby's.

She lived in the left-hand half of a small duplex. The door was unlocked, and Marshall walked right in without knocking as if he lived there. The first thing I noticed were the books. Every wall I could see was lined floor to ceiling with shelves full of books. There were books stacked on the floor in piles of varying degrees of neatness. Libby greeted us with a big "Hi, you guys" from where she sat on the hardwood floor, smoking a cigarette and tapping the ashes into a Tab can, which sat on a copy of *Uta Hagen on Acting*. Across the tiny living room from her was a huge old couch with a pale pink chenille bedspread thrown over it. On the couch were two guys I guessed to be a little younger than Marshall, but obviously older than me. One was thin, vaguely Latin-looking, with Caesar Romero's mustache, Bette Davis's eyes, and Gene Tierney's overbite; the other was hugely fat, bigger even than Libby, and (clichéd though it may be) very jolly-looking. Bald nearly to the crown of his head, he looked like a Caucasian Buddha, or a young Sidney Greenstreet with the giggles.

"Marshall, darling," the Latin one said—almost *sang*, in fact, "what have we here?" He gestured in my general direction with a long, tapering hand.

"Who is she?" the humongous one said.

"Who was she?" the Latin chimed in.

"Who does she hope to be?" they said in unison.

"Put a lid on that shit, will you guys?" Libby said with a toss of her head. "We don't want to scare the boy away right off the bat."

"No, we *cer*tainly wouldn't want *that*," the Latin guy said, with a long, hissy esss sound on the word 'certainly.'

"Cut it out, Raoul," Marshall said. And from the look on his face and the tone of his voice, I could tell he was a little irritated, maybe a bit embarrassed by Raoul and his buddy. What he didn't know was that, as far as I was concerned, I'd just died and gone to heaven. Because, unless my eyes and ears were playing some funny tricks on me, these two guys had to be gay. They talked and acted like every un-funny fag imitation I'd ever seen and forced myself to laugh at. They quoted *The Boys in the Band*. And unless I was mistaken, the big one was giving me a pretty obvious once-over. Here I'd thought I was the only one in town, and here I seemed to have fallen into a buzzing hive of them. I felt like Lassie, and I'd just come home.

"Really, you guys, you just can't turn the shit off for a minute." Libby shook her head like a miffed mom. "Johnnie Ray Rousseau"—Libby indicated the Latin on the couch—"this is Raoul Miranda."

"Carmen's younger, and uglier, sister," chimed the big guy.

"And Arnold Rosenfeld."

"Better known as the Incomparable—Lily Sabina." At which point Arnold Rosenfeld sprang from the couch, struck a Lillian Gish posture and recited in a harsh falsetto: "Oh Oh Oh! Six o'clock and the master's not home yet. Pray God nothing serious has happened"—Raoul joined in—"crossing the Hudson." Arnold fell back on the couch (Raoul moved just in time to escape being crushed beneath Arnold's impressive girth), and the two of them fell all over each other with laughter.

"Take you two anywhere but out," Marshall said with a big eye-roll.

"Well, get you, Miss Thing!" said Arnold. "Getting awful butch in our old age, are we not?"

"Trying to impress Chicken Delight here, one can only presume."

"Kiss my ass, Raoul."

"Any time, Pocohantas, any time."

"All right, ladies, that's about enough of that." Libby lifted herself from the floor. "Let's get to work."

The first read-through was almost a total loss. Arnold and Raoul could scarcely let a line go by without a wisecrack or a sexual allusion. Things had settled a bit by the second reading. Raoul played the part of Marshall's cellmate, who's also Marshall's punk, his wife-away-from-home, really. And Arnold played the prison guard, a part that asked little except that Arnold look large and menacing, something he did quite well. The part of Billy asked little of me except to look young and innocent and scared—which, if Libby was to be believed, I did quite well. I was somewhat relieved to discover that the rape of Billy takes place offstage, and is only alluded to on.

Still, one element of the plot was that both Marshall's character and Raoul's character set out to seduce me—my character, that is; and as we began penciling in Libby's preliminary blocking, it became obvious that there would be a certain amount of homosexual goings-on in *The Lockup*, most of it to include yours truly. Not the least of which was the jam-up-and-jelly-tight scene between me and Marshall; Libby asked especially that Marshall keep what she called that "crotch-grabbing business, like at the auditions." "Lucky you," crooned Raoul. I wasn't sure if he meant Marshall or me.

The tail end of the rehearsal found Arnold and Raoul sprawled out all over the couch I found them in at the beginning of the rehearsal; Libby sitting cross-legged on the floor (her favorite perch, it seemed); Marshall in the big, lumpy overstuffed armchair that (except for the couch and what was probably once a coffee table) was the living room's only furniture; and I, happy as I could remember ever feeling in my life, sitting on the floor between Marshall's outspread legs. So many times, during so many rehearsals and so many cast parties of so many plays, I'd watched so many boy-girl couples holding hands or lounging around in each other's arms, and I'd felt so jealous, so all alone. And now here I was, sitting between Marshall MacNeill's big, sweat-socked feet (his shit-kicker boots long since tossed into a corner) just as natural as could be. And as Libby gave notes ("Pretty good first rehearsal," she said. Then, shooting Arnold and Raoul a glance, "for the most part"), as Raoul and Arnold giggled like silly elementary-school girls, Marshall tugged playfully at my earlobe, stroked the side of my face and neck. Had an out-of-control twenty-ton Mack truck careened through Libby's place, killing us all, I'd have died a happy man.

At the end of rehearsal, Libby said, "Announcement, kids. Your friend and mine, Marshall Two-Hawks MacNeill has graciously given permission for us to use his place for subsequent rehearsals. We are very grateful for this, both because Marshall has much more floor space than I do, and because my roommate has objected, loudly and long, to the use of this place for rehearsals. Thanks, Marsh."

It seemed understood that Marshall would drive me home. We wished Libby and the boys good night, and just went out to Marshall's car, as natural as could be. As if Marshall MacNeill were my boyfriend. My Boyfriend, I repeated to myself, strong-arming the door open, watching Marshall open his door and palm his hair behind one ear before getting into the car.

"You shouldn't mind Raoul and Arnold too much," Marshall said, wrestling Bob Saab into gear.

"I don't mind them at all." True, they weren't the most professional actors I'd ever worked with, but they certainly weren't boring.

"Well, they can be a bit much sometimes. All that Get you, Girl stuff, you know. I just don't go for it."

I didn't have a reply for that one, and nobody said anything for a couple of stoplights' worth of time.

Then Marshall said, "I was wondering—"

"What?" My head lit up like Christmas Eve. Marshall was going to ask me to stick around after rehearsal Friday night. I knew it. I just knew it.

"I was wondering if, maybe, after rehearsal tomorrow, you

might want to have supper with me. Just hang out a while. Listen to some music, maybe. You think?"

"Sure," I said, hoping I appeared cool and casual, even though I felt like doing the Charleston on top of the car, even though I was grinning the Cheshire Cat grin of the year.

"Great. Good. How about I pick you up at your place tomorrow, okay?"

"You don't have to do that. I can walk it."

"About a quarter till?"

"Sure."

Marshall swatted the radio on, and Lou was singing "Take a walk on the wild side" again; and when the colored girls sang "doot-da-doot-da-doo," I leaned back, closed my eyes, and sang along. I felt good. Real good. Because for the first time in my life, I had a boyfriend, practically. And because I'd decided then and there that on Friday evening, after rehearsal, after supper, I was going to make love with Marshall Two-Hawks MacNeill. Or know the reason why.

When we got to my house, Marshall and I must have set Guinness records for long-term handshakes. We just sat in his front seat with our right hands clasped, staring into each other's eyes, both of us (well, I for sure, and him for practically sure) wanting to kiss good night so bad we were steaming up all of Bob's windows. But we were parked right in front of my folks' house, in the middle of a very well-lit street. So, of course, we couldn't.

CHAPTER
14

I FULLY EXPECTED TO DREAM about Marshall all night long. Instead, I hardly remembered any real dreams at all. But I know I dreamed about Todd. I don't remember any plot to the dream, but I remember Todd, just Todd's face. He looked sad, like he'd looked the last couple of times I'd seen him, and I remember feeling sad for him. And then he looked terrified, and he was screaming, screaming. But it didn't exactly look like Todd's face anymore, but more like a mask of some sort—maybe because I've never actually seen Todd scream in real life. And the dream was silent, so it was like that old painting of the silent scream.

The Todd mask screamed and screamed, and it was more horrible than if I could have heard it. And suddenly I awoke, feeling startled and strange. I looked at the alarm clock next to my bed, saw it was nearly four o'clock, and quickly fell back to sleep.

Following the bacon scent into the kitchen for breakfast, I could hear Mom's voice say, "Well, all we can do is remember them all in prayer. That's right," she was saying into the telephone as I entered the kitchen, "leave it in the hands of the Lord." I reached to take a slice of bacon from the paper-towel-covered plate on the stove, when I felt a sudden blow to my stomach, almost like a fist,

and something in the back of my head said Leslie. I looked at
Mom. Her eyes met mine for a split second, then she looked
quickly away and said into the phone, "I've got to get Johnnie
Ray's breakfast, Hildy." She was talking to Hildy Brooks, our
church secretary and the unofficial chairwoman of the church gos-
sip club. I don't think Mom likes Mrs. Brooks very much—but,
like most women, she likes to get the latest news.

Mom put the phone down and looked at me with a look of
absolute horror on her face.

"It's Leslie Crandall, isn't it?"

"How do you know? Who told you?"

"I don't know. Nobody. What is it?"

"Oh, Johnnie Ray . . ."

"Mom—what?"

"Leslie's dead, baby." Mom walked over to me and touched my
face with her hand, as if quietly thanking the Lord I was still alive.
Her hand smelled of bacon. Then she sat down at the kitchen
table, her hands clasped tightly one in the other. "She's dead.
Yesterday."

"Why? How?" My legs felt weak, and I leaned against the stove.

"She—she tried to . . ." Mom turned her face away from me.
"She was trying to get rid of the baby."

"She tried to abort—"

Mom nodded: "With a—" Her voice fell nearly to a whisper. "A
knitting needle. A *knit*ting needle. Lord ha' mercy today," she said
softly.

"Todd? What about Todd?" In my mind, I could see that
screaming mask.

"He's gone. Just, just gone. They don't even know how he
found out. He just jumped on that motorcycle of his and—" She
shrugged a big helpless shrug. "His mother is half crazy with
worry, and Martha Crandall, poor Martha . . ." Her voice trailed
off.

Then she whipped around to me. "Lord Jesus, Johnnie Ray, what is wrong with you children? What is it?" She looked imploringly into my eyes, as if she somehow believed I had an answer.

"I don't know, Mom." I turned to go.

"Don't you want your breakfast, baby?"

"I'm not real hungry, Mom." What I was was angry. At the world, at this town. At Mom. It had made perfect sense to her to send Leslie Crandall halfway across the country, to hide her in her disgraceful pregnancy. To make both Leslie and Todd miserable, punish them both for loving each other, wanting each other.

I went to the bathroom and splashed cold water on my face, getting my shirt and the front of my pants wet in the process, thinking about Leslie. I'd never thought of her as the smartest girl in the world, but she was nothing if not sweet. I could imagine her thinking, If only I could get rid of this baby, they'll let me go home. I leaned over the sink, and left the water running while I cried.

When I got on the bus, I found Carolann sitting alone in one of the front seats, reading. I was pretty sure it was Carolann, since she was wearing a sort of pinafore number in red plaid, the sort of thing Crystal wouldn't be buried in.

"Carolann." She looked up. I gestured her to follow me further back in the bus. "I need to talk to Crystal."

"You like her better than me, don't you?"

"No. It's not that." Actually, I did like Crystal better. "I just need to talk to her about something, that's all. Please?"

"Did you hear about Leslie Crandall?"

"Yes, Carolann, I heard about it. Could I please talk to Crystal?"

"All right." Carolann closed her eyes; when she opened them, it was Crystal. Funny: I was beginning to see where they actually looked different. She said Hi, then looked down at herself. "God, I hate this dress."

"I suppose you've heard what happened to Leslie Crandall."

"Sure. The whole town knows."

"Look, I have to tell you about something: I got the weirdest feeling this morning. Actually, it started last night." I told Crystal about my Todd screaming dream. "And when I heard my mom on the phone, I knew it was about Leslie. Not like a guess or anything. I knew. Do you think it's—"

"Yeah." Crystal nodded. "That'll happen. Don't be surprised. Just let yourself be open to it, and you'll probably notice it happening more often."

"I don't know if I want it to happen more often. It's a little bit creepy."

"Yeah, I know. You're real worried about Todd."

"Yeah."

"There's not a whole lot you can do."

"I know."

"But that won't stop you from worrying, will it?"

"No."

"Thought not." Crystal put her hand on my knee, and I put my hand over hers. And it felt warm, and good. Like somebody who understands. Like a friend.

Cherie and Efrem met me outside the choir room. Cherie ran up to me, threw her arms around me, and buried her face in my neck.

"I can't believe it," she said, her voice a more intense version of her usual whisper.

"I know."

Efrem and I smiled our hellos over Cherie's head. I put my arm around her, and we walked into the room. Inside, there was almost no music playing. Nearly everyone was talking in hushed tones about Leslie and Todd. Even the Foleys were just sitting with their guitars and absently strumming. Cherie and Efrem and I took our usual perch, but there seemed to be nothing to say. Cherie clutched my arm in silence; every now and then I could hear her whisper, "I just can't believe it."

The whole day was practically a total loss. Not even the teachers could seem to concentrate on anything. All anybody seemed to want to talk about was Leslie's death and Todd's disappearance. I could feel one serious depression coming on, and there was nobody to talk to about it, really, because *everybody* was depressed. Mr. Elmgreen went ahead and held the interlude auditions. I did "Blackbird" with Johnny Foley on guitar, with the understanding that after Todd returned, he'd play for me at the concert. I felt a little better when the whole choir applauded after my song.

"Not bad," Mr. Elmgreen said. "A little low-key, but I think we can make time for it." I smiled. He and I both knew that if he didn't make time, he'd have a riot on his hands.

All in all, I only managed to keep from becoming totally morose by thinking about Marshall. About seeing him again. Having late supper with him. Being held in his arms, and kissing his lips. It got me through the day.

I didn't eat much dinner, both because I was so excited about the evening, and because I knew I'd be eating again after rehearsal.

"What's the matter, baby?" Mom asked. "Don't you feel well?" I'm usually a pretty big eater (though you couldn't tell it from looking at me).

"Just not very hungry, Ma." I took a big bite of pot roast, just to make her feel a little better. "I'll be out a little late tonight," I said, trying to sound cool, as if this were something I do all the time, when actually, I don't go out very much at all. I'm generally much more the stay-home-and-watch-old-movies-on-TV type.

"Oh?" Mom's eyes widened. "And just how late is that?"

"I don't know, Ma. Not very. I'm just gonna hang out with the cast for a while, that's all. It's Friday night."

"Well, Friday or not, I don't want you out until all hours with a bunch of people I don't even know. College people. Probably drinking and heaven knows what else."

"Mother—" I really didn't want to get into a big hassle about this.

"And don't 'Mother' me, Little Mister."

"Clara." Dad, who'd been concentrating on doing away with a heaping plate of food, finally spoke up. "Don't give the boy a hard time. He hardly goes out at all as it is. Son"—he emptied a forkful of potatoes into his mouth, and spoke to me through it—"it's Friday night. Go out with your friends and have a good time. Your mother and I trust you to behave yourself as a Christian young man should, and to get home at a decent hour. Don't we, Clara?"

"Lance—"

"That's right"—Dad cut Mom off before she could finish protesting—"we certainly do. Need money, son?"

"No thanks, Dad." Dad gave me a nice man-to-man wink, and dove back into the mashed potatoes. Dad's all right sometimes.

Anyway, so I parked on the living-room sofa, and pretended to read the movie section of the paper, and waited for Marshall. I recognized the sound of his car before he'd even stopped at our house, and I jumped up from the sofa like it was on fire, before Marshall even beeped the horn.

"That's my ride! Bye, Mom. Bye, Dad. Don't wait up." And I was out of there.

I ran full tilt out to Marshall's car, yanked the door open, and stopped dead in my tracks. The guy at the wheel was barely recognizable as the Marshall MacNeill I'd seen the night before. He'd had his shoulder-length hair cut short, practically a butch. It made his neck suddenly seem much longer, and his ears look like the handles on a bowling trophy. If possible, I thought he was even cuter than before. Marshall smiled,

"Surprise."

"Surprise, indeed."

"I've had my hair long since junior high. It was time for a change. Like it?"

"Yes," I said, climbing into the car.

"You don't have to say you like it if you don't." The old Saab lurched into gear and took off. "Won't hurt my feelings."

"I like it a lot." I grabbed the back of Marshall's newly bared neck, surprising myself at my own boldness. I looked at my watch: only six-forty. I hoped we'd get to Marshall's before anyone else. I wanted to be alone with him for a few minutes before Libby and the others arrived. I wondered if Marshall had any similar thoughts.

"About tonight—" My heart stopped. He was going to cancel on me.

"What?"

"I hope you like lamb chops."

"I love 'em." Actually, I'd never been within arm's length of a lamb chop in my life. Dad hates them, so Mom never cooks them.

Marshall lived within walking distance of Libby, in a building much like hers. As we approached Marshall's house, I could see Libby, a vision in a bright orange caftan, sitting on Marshall's front steps. And I thought, "Oh, well. We've got the whole evening."

CHAPTER
15

MARSHALL'S PLACE HAD EVEN LESS furniture in it than Libby's. The living-room furniture consisted of a huge madras beanbag chair. Period. There was an old compact stereo set against one wall, keeping company with what looked like a couple hundred records, bookended with big bricks. A poster of James Dean was tacked up above the stereo, and a sloppy-looking mobile made of seashells, driftwood, wire, and an old horseshoe clicked and clacked from the ceiling. About a lifetime's worth of books, magazines, and newspapers lay around the hardwood floor. But no television, or dining table—not even a coffee table. Not so much as an old Salvation Army sofa.

Rehearsal ran much more smoothly than the night before. Arnold and Raoul were on much better behavior, and the extra floor space made blocking much easier. I thought it would never end.

When it finally did end, and Marshall's front door closed behind Libby, I was nearly spastic with excitement. As Marshall turned from the door, I fully expected to be swept up into his arms in a passionate Garbo and Gilbert embrace. I rose slightly on tiptoe in preparation for it. Instead, Marshall leaned down, kissed my lips so softly and so quickly I nearly missed it, and said, "I'm glad you're here." Then turned and headed for the kitchen. "Let's start cookin'—I'm starved." I followed reluctantly. I was pretty hungry too. But not for lamb chops.

But lamb chops it was. Marshall really rattled them pots and pans, bopping around his miniscule kitchen, humming along to "How Can I Miss You If You Won't Go Away," by Dan Hicks and His Hot Licks, or Patsy Cline, or Ella Fitzgerald, pausing to wipe his hands on a dish towel and change albums whenever the spirit moved him. I chopped onions and grated cheese, and watched Marshall's behind wiggle while he mashed potatoes and sang "ev'ry picture tells a story, don't it?" He occasionally tossed me a smile or a wink, or a quick pat on the behind, and made me less hungry for lamb chops and more hungry for him with each passing minute.

I ate my first lamb chops sitting cross-legged on Marshall's floor, across an upturned orange crate from him, listening to Charlie Parker and wanting Marshall so bad I could hardly swallow. Afterward, we stacked the dishes in the sink (Marshall said he'd do them in the morning), and I went to the bathroom. I gave my mouth a good rinsing out—I figured it was about time for some serious kissing to start—and when I returned to the living room, there was a Randy Newman album on the turntable, and Marshall was sprawled out in the madras beanbag chair. He looked up at me, and I down at him. And seeing Marshall sitting there, looking so darn good, and in the one and only chair—well, my duty was clear. I took a deep breath, strode across the room to where Marshall sat, and plopped down into the chair between Marshall's outspread legs.

I experienced a moment of tension, wondering if perhaps I hadn't done the right thing. Then Marshall slipped his arms around my waist, and I settled back against him.

"Hi, there," he said, palming my chest.

"Hi." My voice came out soft and breathy; I could hardly believe where I was, what I was doing.

Randy Newman mumbled "you can leeeeve yo hat on" from the old stereo against the wall, as Marshall and I half sat, half reclined in that big old beanbag chair. The beanbag molded around the long curves of Marshall's back, and I made a deep, warm armchair of the space between Marshall's legs. Between the insinuating rasp of Newman's voice, and the feeling of Marshall's big hands tracing great, swirling paths up and down my chest, I was feeling about as glad to be alive as I could remember.

Marshall nuzzled the top of my head; I could feel his breath on my scalp, warm as he exhaled, cool as he sucked in the smell of my hair. He mumbled something that might have been "You smell good."

"What?"

"I'm real glad you could stay."

I snuggled back into Marshall's body; a little giggle of contentment effervesced up from my belly like the bubbles in a 7-Up.

"Me, too."

Marshall's crotch pressed up against my butt. He was hard. I dug the feel of that college-boy boner. I could feel the heat of it even through Marshall's pants and my own. Needless to say, I was hard, too—so hard it hurt. I considered moving one of Marshall's hands from my chest down to the bulge in my pants, then thought better of it. Instead, I lifted Marshall's right hand from my chest, and, humming along with Randy Newman, feigning a nonchalance I did not quite feel, I tugged the hem of my T-shirt out from my jeans, and slipped Marshall's hand underneath my shirt.

Marshall's hand was soft and warm against my belly. He moved it slowly upward and stroked my left pectoral, which, thanks to some serious bench-pressing, had only recently become discernable. He cupped his hand over my heart for a moment, as if checking my heartbeat (which was racing), before taking my nipple between his thumb and forefinger and giving it a gentle little squeeze, causing it to pucker and harden as if I'd gotten a chill, and zapping crazy little yahoo arrows through my entire body. I'd never even considered my nipples before, but I made a quick mental note to consider them later. My back arched, catlike, and my

behind pressed more firmly against Marshall's crotch. A little grunt
of pleasure escaped from Marshall's throat.

"I like your body," Marshall said. By now, both his hands were
underneath my shirt, stretching the daylights out of it, stroking my
chest. "It's so solid. Do you play any sports?"

"Not if I can possibly avoid it."

"How come?"

I sighed a long, cold winter. I really didn't want to go into it. I
didn't want to explain my seemingly inbred abhorrence for team
athletics. Explain the residual bitterness of what seemed like several lifetimes' worth of the special brand of humiliation America
seems to reserve for the nonathletic boy. The exruciation of choos-
ing up teams. The taunts and the namecalling. The sweaty, con-
torted faces I could still see so plainly in my mind's eye, faces full
of shock and outrage that anyone could be so clumsy, so awkward,
such a goddamn little sissy. The hours spent in far right field,
living in abject terror of the occasional left-handed batter, praying
fervently to whatever might be up there that nobody would clout
one my way, because even should the Patron Saint of Sissies render me a miracle and allow me to catch the ball, I knew as well as
I knew my own name that even with my most vigorous, grunting,
everything-behind-it throw, I would only manage to deliver the
ball roughly halfway to first base.

I didn't want to go into the time Janice McIntire, the fat, blowsy
slob of a Baptist wife and mother, who, at a church picnic I hadn't
even wanted to attend, took it upon herself to point out to my dad
(loud enough for the entire assembly—indeed for the entire
county—to hear) that his only son threw a baseball "just like a
girl."

I didn't want to explain.

I didn't want to talk.

I wanted to be kissed.

"I just never got into it," I finally said. "That's all."

"Never?"

"Nope." Could we change the subject please? Could we talk about something pleasant, like war and famine?

"Damn. With a bod like this, I'da thought you were an athlete of some kind."

"Well, I'm not. Is that quite all right?" I said, just a bit too slowly, just a bit too loud.

Marshall slipped his hands from under my shirt like he'd found tarantulas nesting in my navel.

"Hey, I'm sorry," he said, obviously unsure of what he was apologizing for. "I didn't mean anything."

There was an uncomfortable beat of silence.

"I'm sorry," I said. "It's just that—oh, God Bless, this is soooo stupid."

"You just look like an ahtlete, that's all."

"Yeah, yeah, it's just that . . . See, I've started working out this year because, well, because of Coach Newcomb sort of, but really because of—well, not to actually be athletic, of course, because I'm just not. What I really want to be is—well . . ." I very nearly didn't say it. Couldn't say it. I had never admitted it aloud before, and now that I was about to, it sat on the end of my tongue, tasting vain and more than a little silly. I spit it out. "Beautiful. I want to be beautiful, okay?"

"What?"

"You know: beautiful. Like a hunk. Like a jock. I mean, all my life I've watched these guys. Stared at them."

"Who?"

"Jocks." Was the man not listening? "You know: football players and baseball players and whateverball players." I leaned forward, propped up against my knees, talking as much to myself as to Marshall. "God, the energy I have expended envying those guys, wishing I was like them. With their broad shoulders and their muscles and everything. So sure of themselves. Hating them. But wanting them, too. Desiring them, y'know? I mean, I whack my-self raw just thinking about those guys. And I know I'm not like them, I'll never in my life be like them, but I can try to at least look like them. Beautiful."

I leaned back into Marshall's arms, feeling rather as if I had exposed myself in public.

"The end," I said. "Slow fade to black."

"Johnnie Ray," Marshall said after a moment, enfolding me into his arms again, "you are beautiful, you know."

"Sure, Sailor," I snorted in my best Barbara Stanwyck who-needs-ya attitude, "you'd say that now. Now that I've laid bare my scarred little soul, and made an utter and complete spectacle of myself, I'm sure you feel quite sorry for me." Then I was Bette Davis. "Well, I don't want your pity."

"Anybody ever tell you you can't take a compliment for shit?" And he jabbed his fingers into my belly.

I let out a western-movie wild-Indian war-whoop to make any of our respective Native American forebears proud, and leaped out of Marshall's arms, landing sh-bap on the floor.

"Don't ever *do* that," I said between gasps. "I am *so* ticklish."

"Oh, *are* we, now?" Marhsall grinned fiendishly, his face a Lon Chaney grotesque, and crawled toward me on all fours, affecting a ghoulish laugh.

I crawled away backward, crab-style.

"Marshall . . . Marshall, don't. Just don't!" Marshall ap-proached, slowly, slowly. "Marshall, don't you dare"—I began to giggle in anticipation—"just don't you—"

And he was all over me, with six or seven hands and about a hundred tickling fingers, all over my chest and belly and armpits. I was soon completely helpless, laughing and shrieking and gasping for breath. I attempted in vain to fend off Marshall's surprise at-tack, but was soon too weak with laughter to struggle. As I screamed and wept and nearly hyperventilated, Marshall suddenly stopped.

I lay on the floor, Marshall sitting straddling my waist, my eyes closed, trying to catch my breath, every now and then a leftover giggle leaking from between my lips.

I felt the warmth of Marshall's breath on my face, and opened my eyes just as he kissed me for the second time, very softly, on the lips.

I lay back in what I hoped was a passable take-me-I'm-yours Rita Hayworth attitude, and waited for Marshall to sweep me up into his arms and carry me into his bed. But when I opened my eyes again, Marshall was looking down at me, the corners of his lips lifted in a little smile.

"You're beautiful," he said, "but you're silly."

And then he was up, and in the kitchen, opening and closing drawers, looking for something.

"If I roll a joint, will you smoke it with me?" he called amid the racket he was raising.

I sat up quickly.

The question had come riding into town out of nowhere in particular, on a beast of questionable pedigree. It caught me off guard. Here my main concern for the evening had been getting Marshall and me out of our clothes and into the nearest bed, and just when I thought maybe we were at last on the same wavelength, Marshall comes up with this.

Who was directing this movie, anyway?

"Uh . . . I've never done that before."

"I thought not." Marshall had located a Baggie containing maybe a couple of tablespoons of pot (I had seen the stuff, been offered it on a couple of occasions—I was in Drama, after all—but had never accepted), and a sieve. "Will you?"

And I thought, God Bless America. I didn't know. Would I?

The reason why I had never smoked the old devil weed before was simple garden-variety fear. Not that I'd ever *really* believed all those anti-drug films they'd been showing since junior high. I had always maintained the possibility that Sonny and Cher had been lying through their imperfect teeth as they extolled the dangers of marijuana. Besides, almost everybody I knew had smoked pot at least once—even some of the Mormons. And none of them had ever jumped out of a fifteen-story window, head filled with smoke and delusions of flight. Not one of them had stepped in front of a speeding double-decker guided-tour bus, thinking himself the god of internal combustion. Or mistaken a gas flame for a chrysanthemum. Or fingerpainted abstract art on walls with his own blood. Or been committed to a quiet, tasteful mental institution, believing himself to be a Lipton flow-thru tea bag.

Obviously, these were mere fictions, myths, and rumors trumped up by the police and the PTA to frighten some of America's more gullible youth away from recreational narcotics. And, in at least one case, they had done their job only too well. For, while I had never been entirely convinced that smoking pot would turn a healthy young man's brain into butterscotch-pie filling, neither had anyone really managed to convince me otherwise.

Suppose (I thought), suppose it only blew the minds of some people and not others? Maybe it had to do with body chemistry or genetics or something. Who was to say that I might not be that unlucky one-in-a-thousand, found in a corner of a sparsely furnished duplex in an inexpensive corner of town, glassy-eyed and drooling, mumbling "I am an orange."

Besides (I had very nearly forgotten), the stuff was illegal. God Bless! I never even jaywalked. Mother of Mercy, what was I getting into here?

What would Ricky Nelson have done?

"Well?" Marshall sat cross-legged on the floor facing me, with the little bag of mossy stuff, the sieve, some cigarette papers, and a saucer on the floor between his sandaled feet, and rolled a paper full of pot between his fingers. (I imagined the reefer and its surrounding paraphernalia, tagged Exhibits A, B, C, and D, after the entire police force burst in and found enough contraband to send us both up the river for a long, long time.)

"Well?" He licked the cigarette closed and slurped the length of it.

Decide decide decide.

Yes! No! I don't know!

"Johnnie Ray"—Marshall stroked a slow figure-eight across the back of my hand with his fingertips—"there's nothing to be afraid of. Really, I think you'll like it."

I looked into Marshall's wide-set deep-brown eyes. He smiled a long, slow one, made a Groucho Marxist gesture with his eyebrows and the joint, and said, "Hey, babe—take a walk on the wild side."

CHAPTER

16

I DIDN'T FEEL ANYTHING, AT FIRST.

"Of course you don't feel anything," Marshall said. "You don't just take the smoke into your mouth and blow it out. Here: take a good, long hit. Take some air in with it. Good. Now, hold it."

I felt a little silly, sitting cross-legged on Marshall MacNeill's hardwood living-room floor, holding in big lungfuls of marijuana smoke, waiting for my mind to blow.

"Okay, now let it out."

I exhaled a smokescreen.

"I still don't feel anything."

"Would you just give it a minute?" Marshall smiled, took the thin, rather inexpert-looking cigarette from my fingers, inhaled with expert-looking tf-tf-tfs, and offered the joint back to me.

"Take another one." I smoked in imitation of Marshall. "You should be comin' onto it pretty soon. This's pretty fair shit." I took in what seemed a goodly amount of smoke, and held it.

Suddenly, I felt my chest expanding, seemingly to bursting, and I coughed and coughed and uncontrollably coughed, and I rolled around on the floor clutching my chest and hacking, and I might have heard Marshall say something about water, and my stomach was spasming and I couldn't breathe, just couldn't catch my breath, and I thought I might throw up, and then Marshall was holding me, trying to hand me a glass of water—it was a Minnie Mouse glass from Disneyland—and I couldn't seem to grip it. Then Marshall was practically feeding me some water. And slowly, slowly, I caught my breath.

As I did, I began to realize that I was feeling rather strange. Off balance. Not quite myself today, thank you.

And Marshall said, "Are you all right?"

And he looked so close, but his voice came from far, far away.

My head felt light as the steam from a cup of hot Nestle's Quik. And my body, oh my my my my body felt all fluffy and fuzzy, like my chest was made of fun fur, and my lungs of cotton candy.

Candy is dandy, I thought, but sex won't—and I giggled a funny little Billie Burke giggle that seemed to come from somewhere across the room.

"Johnnie Ray?"

And he sounded so faaaaar awaaaaaay . . .

"Johnnie Ray, you all right?" Marshall looked more beautiful to me than he had ever looked before. Like he was shot through gauze, like Loretta Young in *The Bishop's Wife*.

I giggled that funny Glinda-the-Good-Witch giggle again.

"What?" Marshall laughed.

"What?" I laughed, at nothing in general and everything in particular.

"I shouldn't say, of course," Marshall said, "but I think you're stoned." I was still laughing.

"Me, too."

"Do you like it?"

"I think so."

I looked around the room. The light seemed not so much light as a glow. It looked as if the evening had been shot in Technicolor by Twentieth Century-Fox, circa 1944. I suddenly thought of *The Gang's All Here*, with Alice Faye and Carmen Miranda; and Bennie Goodman (and his orchestra), who performed a silly song called "Padooka": "If you want to, you can rhyme it with Bazooka."

"Bazooka," I said absently, stroking the cool floor, the wood grain seeming to come alive beneath my fingers.

"What?"

"What?"

Marshall and I lolled about in and around each other's arms, for just how long I could not have begun to guess—time seemed as soft and gooey as Turkish taffy. Marshall got up every year or so to change records. He called on Lady Day. He called on John Coltrane. I was amazed at how clear the music seemed, as if my entire body were made of ears. As if I could not only *hear* the music, but see it dancing along the walls, feel it beat time against my skin.

I sat curled against Marshall's body again, feeling sleep falling down upon me like a thousand cotton balls being dropped from the ceiling one at a time. It occurred to me that perhaps I should ask Marshall to take me home. Except I didn't want to go. Except I wasn't sure if maybe Mom and Dad might still be up, and would be able to tell I was stoned, and both die of heart attacks. Except I still hadn't been to bed with Marshall. I barely heard Marshall say, "It's probably gettin' kinda late."

"Yeah. Yeah, I guess it is."

"I probably should be takin' you home now."

"Yeah. I guess you probably should. I guess."

There was a beat of silence, broken only by the sound of the stereo needle zigzagging aimlessly up and down the butt-end of *Astral Weeks*, and the incessant minor-keyed humming of my brain.

"I don't want to go yet," I said.

"I don't want you to go yet," he said. "I wanted to show you something."

"What?"

"It's in the bedroom."

Marshall's bedroom furniture consisted of one big brass bed (not, I imagined, unlike the one in "Lay Lady Lay"), in an advanced (and probably permanent) state of dishevelment; and that's it. His clothes sat semi-folded in corrugated-cardboard boxes on the floor, or in careless piles in the corners. Marshall kicked aside one such pile with a sandaled foot as we entered the room.

We just stood there at the foot of the bed, me looking up into Marshall's red-rimmed eyes (and he looking down into mine), both of us grinning like a couple of complete morons. Finally, Marshall bent down and kissed me, but really kissed me; his lips just barely parted mine, and his tongue tip wriggled in between them and tickled my gums. Boys and girls, that's all she wrote.

We kissed and kissed, as hard as I wanted, as hard as I could, and nobody said "Hey, not so rough." We kissed until my neck began to hurt from pointing my face upward to meet Marshall's; so Marshall kicked his sandals off, and I pried my sneakers off and stood on Marshall's feet; and we kissed more. His mouth was somehow simultaneously soft and firm, and tasted slightly bitter from the marijuana.

I can scarcely describe the feeling of holding (at last) a man in my arms except to say that I didn't have enough hands to touch him all I wanted. My inadequate pair scurried up and down Marshall as fast as they could, fingering his face, palming his chest, grabbing his ass, then back up again, finger-combing his newly cropped hair. Marshall kissed my lips, my cheeks, my neck; tongued my ears (I stifled a scream with the heel of my hand), licked my nose and bit my chin, and rubbed me as far as he could reach. He massaged my painful hard-on through my jeans, which I took as permission to grab for his. I outlined the thing in Marshall's pants with my fingers, rubbed it up and down with the palm and back of my hand, and Marshall moaned into my mouth. We kissed and rubbed and tugged at each other until we both had to come up for air or suffocate.

"Let's take our clothes off," Marshall suggested through a couple of deep breaths.

"Yeah."

We slithered out of our clothes, arms and elbows bumping in our clumsy attempts to hurry each other's already frantic stripping. Marshall shoved my T-shirt up into my armpits; he traced my pecs with his fingers, making my nipples pucker. I stroked across his shoulders and down his chest (which was smooth as a baby's; even I have a few hairs between my pecs—Marshall had none at all), and rubbed soft circles into his hard belly.

Marshall pulled open the buttons on my jeans, and rubbed my boner through my underwear before reaching in and grabbing it in his hand. The contact made me gasp. I shut my eyes tight and found I couldn't remember a word of the Twenty-third Psalm. I was almost sure I'd shoot all over Marshall's fingers right then and there. And suddenly I thought, what if it's too small? Marshall shoved my jeans and underpants down past my thighs, and I stepped out of them.

"You're beautiful naked," Marshall said, smiling. "I knew you would be." He pulled me to him again and hugged me tight. I pulled away from him and unzipped his pants, and his dick sprang out. It made me think of an arrow—long and straight and big-headed. Almost all my life I'd wondered what it would be like to see and feel another guy's hard dick. And suddenly here was Marshall's, pink and pretty, and hot as a Szechuan sparerib.

"You can hold it," Marshall said. I took it in my hand and squeezed it hard. I could hardly believe I was holding a man's hard penis in my hand. I stroked Marshall's dick up and down, feeling it pulsate in my hand, noticing how his foreskin made for a looser feeling than stroking my own; watched a drop of wet, shiny liquid the likes of which I'd never seen before gather at the tip and fall warm and sticky against my palm. Marshall moaned softly and nuzzled my head, and finally whispered, "Do you want to get in bed?"

"Oh, yeah!"

Being in bed with Cherie Baker had been nice. Really nice. Being in bed with Marshall MacNeill was wonderful. I find it difficult to describe being in bed with Marshall. Both because I get such a feeling just thinking about it (a lump in my throat, and a swelling in my chest, and something of a swelling in my pants, as well) and because I find it difficult to describe the first time I made love with Marshall Two-Hawks MacNeill without using the word "wonderful" constantly.

The feeling of Marshall lying on me in the big brass bed, our bellies rubbing one against the other, hot and slippery, was wonderful. The smell of Marshall's balls, the taste of his sweat on my lips as I kissed his nearly hairless armpit, were wonderful. His long, muscular, completely smooth legs entangled with my legs and the sheets; his stroking my leg with the arch of his foot while

we kissed and clutched and ground our dicks against each other—
wonderful.

You see my predicament.

Marshall crawled down between my thighs and began kissing
my penis, licking it, finally taking it into his mouth; and the word
wonderful suddenly became grossly inadequate. I could hardly believe the feeling. I could hardly stand it. My entire body seemed to
pulsate with excitement and marijuana high. Pleasure zipped
across my body like fingernails across the strings of an Autoharp. I
was solid gooseflesh down to my toes. I couldn't stop moaning.

My dick felt bigger than the Goodyear blimp, and somehow
Marshall was taking the whole thing down his throat, bam bam
bam, again and again and again. His hands were all over me,
stroking and pulling and squeezing, leaving tingling pleasure-trails
wherever they touched. My head filled with music, seemed to fill
the room with a wall of sound the likes of which Phil Spector
never dreamed about; hundreds of orchestras and thousands of
choirs, tuning up and up and up, louder and higher. And a steam
locomotive was chugging faster and faster, and the music got
higher and louder. John Lennon said number nine, number nine,
number nine, and my hips began to move with a life of their own,
and I moaned, and Marshall (from somewhere across the world)
seemed to moan in reply.

The music went higher, and my back arched, arched, arched
well past the point where it should have snapped in two; Leontyne
Price in Valkyrie drag sang an F above high C, while Ginger
Rogers sang Pig Latin, and the orchestras and choirs went higher
and higher, and my dick was too big, it was gonna burst any second, and the music the music the music, and my whole body
spasmed and spasmed and spasmed again, and Marshall held my
hips down on the bed, and my head was bursting and I felt like I
might just explode (not just come, but piss and shit and vomit and

everything, it was all too much). Shirley Temple rolled her eyes and said, "Oh, my goo'ness!"

And I broke apart like a soap bubble, I splattered all over the room, the walls and the ceiling, and someone was screaming screaming screaming, and after a while (a few minutes, a few years), I realized it was me.

And when I woke up—yes, I'm afraid I actually passed out there for a moment or two—Marshall was lying next to me, stroking my face.

"Make no mistake about it," he whispered, "you can really come."

"Thank you." What could I say?

I reached down and took Marshall's penis in my hand; and just held it for a while, somewhat torn between the desire to at least attempt to make Marshall feel as good as he'd made me feel, and the desire just to lie there, holding Marshall's dick and letting him stroke me, for the rest of my life. Finally, I found the energy to crawl down between Marshall's legs.

I discovered, to my pleasure, that I genuinely liked sucking Marshall's cock. Funny thing, because there's nothing worse you can call a guy than a cocksucker. You say "Suck my dick" to most guys, them's fightin' words. Makes you wonder if there isn't something really disgusting about it. So, even though I'd almost always been fascinated by the thought of it, I still hadn't any idea how I'd take to a mouthful of the actuality of it. Still, it had felt so, well, wonderful being on the receiving end of my first blow job, I was determined to do my best to repay Marshall in kind, like it or not: it was only fair. Anyway, as I said, I really liked it, everything about it. I liked the feeling of him in my mouth, the taste of his skin and the funky stuff around his foreskin; the soft, continuous moaning that let me know I was probably doing it right. I even liked the taste of Marshall's come; sort of a sourdough bread flavor, but not quite.

"Was it okay?" I asked afterward.

"My dear," he said somewhat breathlessly, "that was considerably better than okay. Where'd you learn to suck so good?"

"Right here."

"You mean, this was your first?" he raised up on one elbow.

"Yep." He just said wow, and lay back in bed.

We held each other close for a time (who knows how much time) until Marshall grabbed my dick and said, "You're hard again."

"Not again: still." My dick had not even considered the option of going soft since I'd positioned myself in Marshall's lap in the beanbag chair.

"Oh, to be eighteen!" Marshall said, and enjoyed a little laugh to himself. He fingered my balls for a minute before he said, "You know what I'd like?"

"What?"

"I'd really like you to fuck me."

"Wow."

"Want to?"

"Oh, wow, yeah."

"Awrite."

He reached under the bed and pulled out a tube like toothpaste, and a towel. We knelt, and Marshall squeezed a glob of shiny clear gel from the tube and spread it all over my dick. He rubbed my slick penis up and down a couple of strokes, and said (to himself, to me, I don't know), "Boy, this is gonna be nice." I'd always pictured butt-fucking as being done back-to-front, dogs-on-the-lawn fashion; so I was a little surprised when Marshall lay back, grabbed his ankles, and pulled his legs back nearly to the brass headboard. He said, "Go slow."

I went as slow as I could, considering by the time I was all the way inside Marshall, I was so excited I was on the very doorstep of another orgasm almost instantly. I began whispering the Get-

tysburg Address (as well as I could remember it under the circum-
stances), looked up and counted the cracks in the ceiling, did my
level best to concentrate on anything but just how excruciatingly
good it felt. Marshall, for his part, thrashed his head from side to
side, and moaned so loudly I was afraid I might be hurting him.

"Are you all right?" I said.

"Oh, God, yes!"

When we finished, I fell back on the bed, sweaty and spent
and—despite having eaten two dinners—starving.

"Munchies, huh?" Marshall grinned.

"I could eat a horse. A herd of horses."

There was half a Snackin' Cake and an almost-full pitcher of
strawberry Kool-aid in the refrigerator; we consumed it all, sitting
on the kitchen floor in just our pants, making unabashed smacking
sounds as we ate, shoving cake into each other's face like in some
demented gay-wedding picture. I was sucking cake crumbs off my
right hand (and Marshall my left) when it hit me. "Ohmygosh!
What time is it?" I looked up at the art-deco clock hanging over
the stove. "God Bless! It's nearly two." I jumped up off the floor,
suddenly not feeling in the least bit stoned, and headed for the
bedroom in pursuit of my clothes.

"So it's nearly two." Marshall followed me into the bedroom.
"So what?"

"So I gotta go home. My mother's probably having her nine-
teenth nervous breakdown."

"Do you have to go? I mean, couldn't you crash here tonight?"
He touched me on a naked shoulder. "I'd really like you to."

"Boy, I'd really like to. Correction: I'd love to. But I can't. I'm
supposed to be home at a decent hour, which I'm already too late
for." I yanked my sneakers on and stuffed my socks into my back
pocket. "Would you take me home, please."

"Nope."

"No?" I panicked. The buses had long since stopped running, and it would take me at least an hour to walk.

"I was kidding. Of course I'll take you."

I clutched Marshall's thigh all the way home, praying that Mom and Dad weren't still waiting up. I wasn't sure if, upon laying eyes on me, they wouldn't know (by parent telepathy or something) that, far from behaving as a Christian young man should, I had spent the evening using illegal narcotics and engaging in sodomy. Only one living-room lamp was lit when we got to the house, which meant the folks had more than likely gone to bed. It was practically the only light on the whole block. We sat in the car for a few minutes, staring straight ahead, kneading each other's hand. I didn't want to get out of the car. I wanted to go back to Marshall's, climb back into his big brass bed, and sleep in his arms till nearly noon.

"Thanks for spending the evening with me," he said.

"Thank you. I had—it was wonderful. I—" And we were kissing, so hard our teeth clicked against each other.

"Good night, Johnnie Ray."

"Good night, Marshall."

I ran into the house, where Dad's snoring was audible all the way into the living room. Relieved beyond words, I tiptoed into the bathroom and brushed my teeth, staring at my reflection in the mirror, half expecting to look somehow different than I had that afternoon. I'd barely crawled into bed when I heard Mom's voice from across the hall.

"Good night, baby."

"Night, Mom."

Sleep came immediately, heavy and dreamless.

CHAPTER
17

NO MENTION WAS MADE ABOUT my late hours. When I finally made it into the kitchen, around noon, hell-bent for the coffee pot, Mom simply asked if I'd had a good time. I said yes, I'd had a very good time, and that was the end of it. I could only imagine Dad had asked her not to play Spanish Inquisition with me about it. Actually, I would have loved to be able to tell Mom about Marshall. Or tell Efrem or Cherie, or anybody. Actually, Cherie might have been all right, except considering how she felt about me, it might not be the kindest thing to talk to her about. Then I thought, Crystal. I could probably talk to Crystal about it, tell her everything. Of course, knowing her, she would probably be able to tell *me* about it.

I wasn't good for much the whole day. My head was a little foggy, and what little conscious thought I managed was mostly about Marshall. I stayed in my room most of the day, working on a macramé wall-hanging I'd been poking at for weeks, listening to the stereo, finally watching *Stage Door* for the umpteenth time on the late show. About the only time I emerged was for food or the bathroom, and five or six times to call Marshall, just to hear his voice. There was no answer at his place.

Sunday, and church was even emptier than the week before. Pastor and Mrs. Crandall had flown back east—they'd decided to bury Leslie there instead of bringing her back. Daniel Levine, our assistant pastor and youth minister, was preaching, which usually thinned the congregation pretty well all by itself. Daniel is a Jew who's only recently converted to Christianity; and, while he is possessed of all the religious fervor one would expect, he's just not much of a speaker. Anyway, the energy was a little strange in the sanctuary, what with Leslie's death, the Crandall's absence, and the fact that Todd Waterson was still missing. I'm sure all these things were mentioned, at least alluded to, in Daniel's sermon, but (to tell the truth) I don't remember a word of it. My head was full of Marshall MacNeill.

I called him up after church, but there was no answer.

I did decide to tell Crystal about Marshall, in excited but hushed tones at a back-corner table in the library, right before getting thirty-nine out of fifty-two with the cards (I'd been stalled at forty or so for days—I couldn't seem to get any better).

"Well, good for you," Crystal said. "I love love, myself. Can I give you a piece of advice, though?"

"Sure."

"Don't ask more of this thing than there really is."

"What do you mean?" Don't say nothin' bad about my baby.

"Just don't get yourself hurt, okay?"

"Is this some sort of prediction?"

"No. Just some free advice, that's all."

I didn't hear from Marshall until Wednesday evening after dinner. I'd been calling his place four or five times a day, from the pay phones at school and from home after. I pounced on the phone somewhere in the middle of the first ring, as I'd been doing consistently since Saturday night.

"Hello?"

"Johnnie Ray? This is Marshall MacNeill."

I had previously resolved that, when I heard from Marshall, I was going to be very cool, very Katharine Hepburn self-sufficient, let him know I no more required the sound of his voice for survival than he required mine.

"Hello." I had a feeling I sounded less like Hepburn than like a pouting child.

"Hi. How are you?"

"Fine." Just ginger peachy, Mr. Part-Cherokee; just strong and healthy and (oh, by the way) stark, raving nuts about you, and where the Sam Hill have you been since Saturday night, doggone ya? "And yourself?"

"Fine."

"That's fine."

"You sure you're all right, Johnnie Ray? You sound funny. Was it a bad idea to call?"

"No. I'm fine, really. So where—what've you been doing?"

"Editing, constantly. I've been at school, editing my film every day since, well, since I saw you last. I'm supposed to show it next Saturday."

"You've been at the college all day?"

"All day. It's pretty hard word. You're not making it any easier."

"What do you mean?"

"I mean, it's hard to concentrate when I can't get you out of my mind. I've missed you." Needless to say, that was all it took to melt me like so much ice cream in the summertime. I smiled so wide so fast I nearly pulled a muscle in my face.

"I've missed you, too."

"Good. Two things: *a*, you are coming to see my film next Saturday. That's not a question—you have no choice."

"Well, that settles that."

"And *b*, the play's off."

"*The Lockup?* How come?"

"Because Libby's directing teacher got wind of what she was doing, and deepsixed it right quick. She'd told him it was going to be *The Bald Soprano*. He's still deciding whether to let her come up with another idea before the end of the semester or just give her a great big "Not Pass" and get it over with. So, anyway, it's off."

"Oh. When will I see you?"

"I was kinda hoping for Thursday. I mean, your folks are expecting you to go to rehearsal Thursday and Friday, right?"

"Right."

"So, come on-a my house."

"You gonna give me candy?"

I heard Marshall chuckle to himself.

"I'm gonna give you everything."

CHAPTER

18

I AM ASHAMED TO ADMIT THAT, notwithstanding my newly discovered psychic powers (such as they are), I had not so much as a hot flash at the time of Efrem's "accident." Not a glimmer. Zilch. Not until after it was all over. Crystal explained to me later that even the most experienced, most talented psychics had lapses; that someone who, like me, was just beginning to feel out his psychic energy couldn't very well expect to know every time somebody they care about is in trouble. Then what friggin' use is it, I asked her. You're just upset, she said.

Anyway, what happened happened on Saturday afternoon, while I sat in the film theater at the J.C., enduring what seemed an endless program of horrendous student films, waiting for Marshall's film, hoping to heaven that *it* wasn't going to be horrendous, too. I'd managed to arrive late (not knowing where the film theater was), and I was pretty sure I could see the silhouette of Marshall's head in the front row. Most of these films were quite beyond my comprehension: one was seven minutes of various people's bare feet. Now, I like feet as much as the next guy, but an entire short subject? Another one had two people, a man and a woman, engaged in a conversation that I don't think anyone was meant to understand, all in extreme (and I mean extreme) close-ups of their mouths. Yet another featured a middle-aged man sitting on the toilet reading *U. S. News and World Report* while a large horsefly buzzed around the bathroom. I thought, If this is Film, I'll take Movies anytime, thank you.

Marshall's Film (he always spoke of it in the upper case) was last on the program. I crossed my fingers as it flickered into view. It began with a piece of an old, dog-eared theater trailer, the one with an animated-cartoon trio composed of a hot dog, a soft drink, and a box of hot buttered popcorn, all truckin' across the screen, singing "It's intermission, it's intermission." Then the action (and I'm using the term loosely here) quick-cuts to a nondescript kitchen with a nondescript dinette set, at which sit two hugely obese, completely naked people—a man and a woman—who (I immediately realized) looked strangely familiar to me. On the dinette table are a couple of open-faced hamburgers; the table is crammed with condiments. It wasn't until the woman jammed a butter knife into an economy-size jar of Best Foods (Real) Mayonnaise and began to spread it vigorously onto her hamburger bun that I realized that the woman was in fact Libby, and the man Arnold (The Incomparable Lily Sabina) Rosenfeld. My mouth fell open so wide my chin hit me in the chest.

As the "It's Intermission" jingle played over and over in the background (and believe me, they could use this thing to torture prisoners of war), Libby and Arnold (naked as the day they were born) smear these big hamburgers with mayo and relish, pile on the onions and lettuce, and proceed to eat these burgers with lip-licking, eye-rolling gusto; red-and-white rivulets of sauce trickled down their chins and onto their breasts (Arnold's easily rivaling Libby's for pendulous size).

I slid down in my seat, both hands clamped over my mouth, wondering what in the world I was going to say to Marshall about this, this *thing* I was being forced to witness. Much to my surprise, the audience (maybe thirty people in all—undoubtedly Marshall's classmates and their friends) neither laughed aloud, hooted, nor pelted the screen with decomposing vegetable matter. On the contrary, they seemed to be watching the Film with critical care; indeed, they seemed to be taking this thing seriously. Marshall's Film ended with close-ups of Libby and Arnold's ketchup-smeared faces, smiling in gluttonous glee, as the words "It's Intermission" crackled through the sound system one last time.

The audience burst into spontaneous applause as the house lights clicked abruptly on, causing momentary blindness, at least for me. Marshall stood up from his seat in the front row (with the other student filmmakers), smiled, and took a short bow. I watched people rise from their seats and bee-line to the front row. I overheard a young woman say to her companion, "He's symbolized the conspicuous overconsumption of Western society so perfectly." Now, it never would have occurred to me that a seven-minute short subject of naked fat people eating hamburgers might be symbolic; still, I found myself saying "conspicuous overconsumption of Western society" softly to myself, in case I was strapped for something to say to Marshall.

When I reached the front of the theater, Marshall was in an intense-looking conversation with an equally intense-looking thirtyish man in thick eyeglasses and a sweatshirt. Various people from the audience walked up and pumped Marshall's hand or slapped his back as he talked—he seemed to be the hit of the afternoon. He caught me out of the corner of his eye and tossed me a quick smile before turning back to the guy in the glasses, who was saying "major stepping-stone in your career, something that'll look damn good on your resumé," and blah blah blah. Marshall said, "Right back, okay?" and Mr. Glasses said "Tha's cool," and Marshall turned to me.

"Hi."

"Hi." He took my shoulder and led me to a less populated corner of the theater.

"I'm glad you came. When you weren't here when the lights went down, I wasn't sure. What'd you think of my Film?"

"I thought it perfectly symbolized the conspicuous overconsumption of Western society." What the hey, why waste a good line?

"Wow! I'd have thought you were too young to pick up on the symbolism. You're real sharp."

"Are we still on?" We'd made plans to go to Marshall's place again for a bit of the old slap-and-tickle after the Films.

"No, I'm afraid not."

"No?" The thought crossed my mind that he was going to slap-and-tickle the guy in the glasses, but (without being mean) this guy was no looker, so I ruled that one out. "How come?"

"See that guy I was talking to? He's second-crew director on a new western that's gonna be shot out in Arizona. His assistant just crapped out on him, and he's talking about giving me the job. He liked my Film and he's sort of a friend of Libby's. Anyway, he wants to talk about it right away. So I've got to cancel out. You understand, don't you? This could be a major stepping-stone in my career."

"Look great on your resumé," I said, sarcasm seeping out from between my teeth.

"Don't be mad, Johnnie Ray." Marshall took me by the shoulders. "Please. I really need to do this. I'll call you soon, okay? I promise. Okay?"

"Okay."

"Thanks. Wish me luck."

"Good luck."

"Thanks. And thanks for coming to see my Film. See ya later." And he hurried off.

I bused it home, disappointed for sure, wondering what I was going to do with the rest of my afternoon, but feeling all right overall. When I walked in, Mom was in the kitchen, talking on the phone.

"Oh, Lord, Shirley, I know how you must feel," she was saying. "It would just about kill me. I—" She noticed me. "I gotta go, Shirley, Johnnie Ray's home, call me when you get home." She put the phone down like it was on fire. "Hi, baby."

"Hi, Mom. What's going on?"

"I was just talking with Shirley Johnson. She's over at the hospital. Efrem's had an accident."

That's when I felt it. Cold. A chill to my bone marrow, on a warm afternoon.

"What? What happened?"

"He . . ." Mom averted her eyes. "He fell."

"Fell?"

"Down some stairs."

"Oh, Mom!" I reached for the door.

"Oh Mom, what?"

"The Johnsons live in a one-story house. I'm going to the hospital."

"Johnnie Ray—" And I was out of there. I dug my old three-speed out of the garage (I hardly ever ride it—around here, if you must ride a bike, it had better be a ten-speed) and pedaled off toward the hospital. I tried to think what it could be about Efrem's accident (whatever it was) that would make Mom suddenly become this teller of tall tales. Maybe Efrem had been driving drunk and broke both his legs or something. Maybe it had something to do with drugs or a girl or—or a guy. The thought rang true from the second it grazed my mind. It was a guy. I would have bet my last dime. I pedaled furiously.

The receptionist at the hospital was doing a crossword puzzle. "Efrem Zimbalist Johnson."

"What?" She looked up. She had one of those sour faces that look like its owner just stepped ankle-deep in doggie-doodie.

"Efrem Zimbalist Johnson—what room is he in?" She glanced down at the desk.

"Room 101, but this isn't visiting hours." I started down the hall. "Hey," she called after me. "You, boy—come back here!" I stepped up my pace; I could hear the receptionist mutter "Dog-gone-it" to herself, and then the squeaky-squeak of her sensible white shoes down the hall behind me. I found room 101 and opened the door without bothering to knock.

The very first thing I saw was Efrem, propped up in the bed, facing the door. My eyes seemed to work like a telephoto lens, zooming in for an unrelenting close-up of Efrem's face; it was swollen almost beyond recognition. His left eye was completely shut. The right one opened wide as Efrem caught sight of me. His lips were so fat they seemed to be crowding his nose; his skin was bruised a mottled purple.

I felt as if the heavyweight champion of the world had just slugged me his best shot right to the stomach, the wind was knocked out of me, and I felt sick. "I *told* you to stop." The receptionist had walked up and grabbed me by the arm. "Now you just come with me."

"That's all right." Mrs. Johnson was standing by Efrem's bed. She clutched a wadded handkerchief in one hand; her eyes were red and puffy from crying. She'd obviously been there all along, and I hadn't even seen her. "He can stay."

"But these aren't regular visiting hours." The receptionist still hadn't let go of my arm. "Till eight o'clock, this room is restricted to the boy's immediate family."

"It's all right," Mrs. Johnson said. "This is his brother."

"His—" The receptionist looked at me, then at Mrs. Johnson, then rolled her eyes and did a little shrug, and finally let go of my arm. "All right, go on then," she said half over her shoulder as she turned and walked away down the hall.

"Thanks, Mrs. Johnson."

"Come on in, Johnnie Ray." Mrs. Johnson started toward the door. "I'll be in the hall, honey," she said to Efrem, who still hadn't uttered word one.

"You don't have to leave, Mrs. Johnson," I said.

"I'll be right outside the door," she said. "Right in the hall."

The door shut behind me, and I walked toward Efrem's bed. Efrem's swollen lips barely parted enough for him to say hi.

"Who did this?"

His good eye shut tight, and a tear fell from the corner of it.

"Fell."

"You did not *fell*, Efrem." I was sure of that much. "Who beat you up, baby?" Eyes still shut, Efrem shook his head from side to side, over and over, no no no no no. I took his hand (clenched into a fist in front of him) and squeezed it hard.

"Please, Efrem."

His head stopped shaking and fell back against the pillows. Efrem took a deep, shaky breath and whispered, "Dad." Tears coursed down his swollen face.

"Oh, God."

Slowly, haltingly, with some difficulty through the swelling of his mouth, Efrem told me the story: Efrem's parents had gone out visiting for the day, supposedly all day. Instead, they'd returned early.

"They went to my room. Found me. In bed. With. Somebody."

I took a chance. "With a guy."

He nodded, weeping. A violent shudder passed through me. Efrem didn't even have to tell me the rest. It was only too easy for me to imagine Efrem's father, a big handsome James Garner type, walking in on Efrem and whoever the guy was, and just going berserk. Beating his own son to a bloody pulp, doing God only knew what to the other guy. I began to cry, too. For Efrem, and for myself.

"How did you know?"

"I guess I always sort of knew. I'm gay, too."

"I always thought . . . maybe . . . I was scared."

"To tell me. I know, baby. I was scared to tell you, too." I pressed his hand again. "Who was the guy?"

"John. I met him . . . at the library." In the music stacks, among the musical-comedy scores—Efrem plays the piano; he loves Rodgers and Hammerstein. Seems Efrem and this guy had been meeting whenever they could catch a moment together, for over a month. "When we heard the car in the drive, John tried to get away." The Johnsons came into Efrem's bedroom just as John was climbing out the window, his pants barely zipped.

"He called me faggot." Efrem screwed the heel of his hand into his unswollen eye. "He kept saying it—faggot, goddamned little faggot—while he hit me. It wasn't the hitting that hurt so much, it was the names."

There was nothing I could say to console him, nothing I could do to help. I stroked Efrem's hair and tried to stop crying.

"When are you going home?"

"I don't know. Maybe never." He stopped rubbing his eye and looked me in the face. "I've got to get out of this town."

"I know, baby. I know."

Mrs. Johnson met me just outside the door; she clasped my arm tightly.

"He told you, didn't he?"

"Yes."

"You mustn't tell anyone, Johnnie Ray. Promise me you won't tell."

"I won't tell anybody, Mrs. Johnson." I was pretty sure I wouldn't have to.

When I got home, I could hear Mom and Dad talking in the den over the sound of an "I Love Lucy" rerun. It wouldn't have taken a psychic to guess what they were talking about, even without hearing the words.

I picked up the phone and dialed Marshall's number. After thirteen rings, I finally put it down. Then I went to my room and put on Joni.

I was right about one thing. By Monday morning the whole school knew Efrem Zimbalist Johnson's father had messed up Efrem's face over the weekend. No one seemed any too clear as to just why Mr. Johnson might want to beat the shit out of his only son, although the best and most colorful guesses tended to involve sex. (The one most frequently bandied about, naturally, was that Efrem had knocked up some girl.)

As I suspected, word had (at least partially) got out; and with no help whatsoever from me. Around here, if one person knows something at breakfast time, the whole damn town's heard it by noon. Maybe the version that hits the street is a few generations removed from the truth, but it's probably not so far away that there isn't some family resemblance. Knowing this to be the case, I took a big chance (sort of a calculated risk born of desperation) when I told Skipper, and then Cherie, that I'm gay. The chance that neither of them might ever want to see or hear from me again, of course; and the (perhaps more serious) chance that one or both of them might tell the butcher, the baker, the candlestick maker, or maybe even (horrors!) my parents that Johnnie Ray Rousseau is as queer as they come.

Not that it would have occurred to me to fear actual bodily harm from the very people who gave me life. On the other hand, neither was I so naive as to suppose I could simply march up to

Mom (standing by the stove stirring roux gravy and singing "In the Sweet By-and-By" softly to herself) and say, "Excuse me, Mom, but I just wanted you to know I'm a homosexual," and expect her to say "That's fine, baby; dinner be ready soon."

After all, I've known about me for a long time now. Even before I knew there was a word (several words, in fact) for a boy like me, who finds that his love light shines brightest on other boys, I knew I was different; and I was at least semi-comfortable with that fact by the time I was thirteen or fourteen years old. And with the knowledge that there are indeed others, that in L.A. there are lots and lots of others just waiting to be located, came the desire, indeed the immediate life-goal to escape to (as Joni once called it) the City of the Fallen Angels while my high-school diploma was still hot in my hands—to bid this tight-assed little town ta-ta, returning only for the occasional weekend, lest the parental purse strings be pulled prematurely shut.

Oh, I had every intention of telling the folks the truth about me—in due time. Like in the mid-Eighties, following graduation from the University, once I was firmly established in my singing career and quite financially independent, thank you. It's not as if I considered my parents child-eating ogres or anything. It's just that Mom and Dad haven't had nearly the time to adjust to the idea of my being gay that I've had. So why push it, you know? And if by some chance they did find out (and, as I say, I always knew there was that chance)—well, I'd just have to cross that bridge when I got to it. I just sort of hoped I wouldn't get to it.

Now, Efrem's "accident" made the thought of being found out by the folks infinitely more frightening than it had ever been before. The possibility of a fate similar to Efrem's befalling yours truly was one ugly possibility, indeed. In terms of muscular strength, my dad makes Efrem's dad look like a ninety-seven pounder. My face might never be the same. So between my best buddy (now my best gay buddy) having had his nose relocated by

his own father, and my renewed fear of discovery, the days following the Accident found me in a serious funk. My head was so full
of depression, that my psychic abilities had regressed to the point
where I was no longer getting a statistically significant number of
cards right. Crystal assured me it would pass. School seemed endless; I couldn't concentrate in class, and I couldn't seem to study
worth a damn afterwards, and finals loomed large on the horizon.
I was pretty sure I'd get by; but then, just getting by has never been
my style.

Not exactly helping through this trying time was the fact that
Marshall was gone. I mean real gone. I must have called him
thirty-seven times that Saturday after leaving Efrem in the hospital, knowing just hearing his voice would help. No reply. I dou-
bled that number on Sunday, to no avail. Monday looked much
the same. Tuesday, I got a recording: the number I had dialed was
no longer in service. A lump the size of the library's world globe
grew in my throat and spent the day. Finally, on Wendesday, I got
a letter postmarked Prescott, Arizona, written on one sheet of lined
paper ripped out of a spiral notebook:

Dear Johnnie Ray:
    So sorry for not getting in touch by phone. The past few days
have been insane. I left for Arizona Saturday night, and I've been
working on this film—correction—this movie, ever since. It's been
wild.
    It's been real special, Johnnie Ray. You're real special. Never
forget that. Take care. Have a good summer. Good luck at
U.C.L.A., not that you'll need it.
    I know we'll see each other again.

                    Love,
                    Marshall Two-Hawks MacNeill

My first reaction was tears. I needed Marshall Two-Hawks Mac-
Neill, needed him here and needed him now. How dare he not be

here? My second reaction was to rip the letter to shreds and toss them into the kitchen garbage pail. My third reaction was to dig the shreds out of the kitchen garbage pail and Scotch-tape them back together, and tuck the reassembled letter into my three-ring binder.

Anyway, one thing and another, I'd had better weeks. And hanging over the proceedings like hail-bearing clouds was the nagging, nearly relentless sense of foreboding, a feeling that something unbearably ugly was due to happen to me soon.

CHAPTER
19

IT HAPPENED ON A SATURDAY night, two weeks to the day after the Accident. I'd been out at the J.C.; Skipper had asked me especially to come and see *Hooray for Love*. How could I say no? I suppose (as Mom would say) I just watch too many old movies, but I must admit to feeling a pang or two as I walked down the selfsame hall where I first saw Marshall, walking that bow-legged big-assed walk of his.

The play was everything I'd expected. In fact, parts of it weren't even as *good* as "Love American Style." The Romeo and Juliet scene was a little bit painful to watch; Skipper and Kathleen ended up doing it, and they weren't bad at all. It's just that I'd have killed to do that scene. Afterward, I went backstage to do the big Congratulations, Dahling number; made a big deal out of shaking hands with Brock, watching him wince at my approach, probably wondering if I planned to uproot one of the seats and bean him with it; declined an invitation to the cast party—I mean, who needs that shit?—and bused it home.

Approaching the house, starting up the driveway, I suddenly got the overpowering urge to turn on my heels and just keep walking, all the way to L.A. maybe. This was it, I thought, the moment we'd all been waiting for. I took a deep breath and went in.

My ugliest fears had come true, and were sitting in the living room. Mom sat bolt upright on the sofa, wearing a look of complete and utter disgust; a look just a scream away from infanticide; a look that could turn a seventeen-year-old boy to stone. Dad sat next to her, his face buried in his hands, weeping audibly, his massive shoulders shaking with sobs. I'd never seen my father cry before, not even at his father's deathbed. The sight of it now was another Mohammed Ali right hand to my stomach.

Across from my parents, literally on the edge of the chair, sat Daniel Levine, youth minister of our church. At the sight of Daniel's slightly cross-eyed, perpetually five-o'clock-shadowed face, I suddenly remembered something I must have subconsciously forced myself to forget. Something that, upon remembrance, made my heart slam on its brakes and screech to a stop. I remembered that I had not only told Cherie Baker and Skipper Harris that I was homosexual, I had also told Daniel Levine.

It happened several months previous to that black Saturday night. I had just seen *The Exorcist* down at the drive-in with Efrem and a carful of the Drama II gang. Kathleen spent most of the movie with her hands over her eyes; Skipper, who had made off with a six-pack from his house, drank five of the six and ate his share of the large pepperoni pizza we bought at the snack bar and then (concurrently with Linda Blair spewing hot guacamole all over Max von Sydow) opened the car door and barffed his guts out all over the pavement. Efrem loved the movie, start to finish.

Of us all, only I seemed to have been moved to a profound

sense of spiritual guilt. The following day, I paid Daniel Levine a visit, and confessed that I thought I might be homosexual, half out of a sudden fear of eternal damnation (or terrestrial demonic possession at the very least), half out of the wild hope that Daniel might assure me that the Lord loved me just as I was.

What Daniel did was wrinkle his one great eyebrow and assure me (clearing his throat every few words) that I was indeed not a homosexual at all, but that Satan had planted this wild notion in my mind to test the steadfastness of my Christian commitment.

"Satan will often suggest (ahem) certain ungodly desires to the minds and hearts of Christian young people," said Daniel, avoiding my eyes and wiping his palms on the tops of his thighs. "You haven't (cough, cough) acted on these desires, of course?"

I assured Daniel that I had indeed not yet acted upon these desires, of course (omitting the fact that this was entirely due to lack of good opportunity). Daniel then proceeded to lay hands on me and pray for my speedy deliverance from these unnatural and ungodly desires, instructed me to pray likewise daily, assured me that of course this entire matter was strictly between the two of us, and sent me on my way. It was maybe a day and a half before I was completely over the notion that my gayness was inherently evil or ungodly; and the fact that I'd ever even spoken with Daniel Levine never again entered my mind.

That is, until I suddenly found myself confronted with the unpleasant spectacle of Daniel, obviously having spilled the old beans to Mom and Dad, and looking as holy and righteous at having done so as my parents looked utterly devastated at the news. All three heads turned as I shut the front door behind me.

Dad wept. Mother glowered. Daniel—amazingly—smiled.

"Hello, Johnnie Ray," he said. "We've been waiting for you."

I could scarcely believe this was happening. It was as if the world was coming to an end with both a bang and a whimper. I took a seat across from Mom and Dad. Mom sat ramrod stiff, with a Gale Sondergaard sort of a sneer on her face; Dad looked as if he hadn't slept in a week of nights, his eyes bright red from crying.

"You probably know why I'm here, Johnnie Ray," Daniel said, the picture of calm. He could afford to be calm. He wasn't watching his life being blown to smithereens like Krakatoa East of Java. "What with what happened to Efrem Zimbalist Johnson, I thought it the better part of valor to check in on you, find out how you were doing vis-à-vis your"—he avoided my eyes—"your sexuality. I informed your mom and dad that you'd come to me with a problem. A problem with unnatural desires."

"You said it was between us."

"I know, Johnnie Ray; I know I did. But I just felt that, in light of the . . . the incident with Efrem, that perhaps parental involvement was in order. I'm sure you understand."

"I'm sure," I said with all the sarcasm I could muster.

"Good. Tell me"—Daniel studied his knees—"have you continued to experience these, these unnatural desires?"

Here it was: the bridge I'd told myself I would cross when I got to it. My stomach felt like lead. I took a deep breath.

"Yes. And I've accepted them. I'm gay."

Dad began to cry with renewed vigor. Mom's sneer curled further.

"You probably think you're real cute," she said, "going to Daniel with this 'I think I'm a homosexual' crap, and now sittin' here and tellin' us you've *accepted* that you're gay."

"No, Mother I don't think—"

She clamped her fist over her belly.

"Lord ha' mercy today! I don't know what I coulda done to give birth to a per*vert*."

"Mother, I am not a pervert." I hated the way my voice sounded: weak and whiney and childish.

"You are! Per*vert*!"

Dad sobbed out loud. Mom put a hand on his heaving shoulder and shot me a crippling glance.

"Mom . . . Mother . . ." I could hear my own voice breaking, feel tears hot behind my eyes. "I can't help what I am." I tried so hard to speak calmly. I didn't want to sound like some hysterical child, even though I felt exactly like some hysterical child. "And I am gay."

Dad wailed again. Mom's eyes narrowed to shiny slits.

"You're doing this to hurt us!" she accused.

"No!" I'd never in my life felt so helpless, so weak. How could I cause this kind of pain, just by being what I am? I wasn't trying to hurt anybody. God, I was just trying to be. "No. I love you."

"You don't."

"Mother!"

"You can't. Say you love us, and then do somethin' like this."

"Mother." I was crying by this time, just couldn't hold it back. "It's not something I'm doing. It's something I am. I just *am*."

"It's wrong, Johnnie Ray. God don't like it. It's dirty and sinful and it's just plain wrong."

I felt nauseated; I thought I might vomit.

"It's of Satan, Johnnie Ray. You have to fight it."

"I can't."

"You can!" she said with a finality that let me know it was from God's lips to hers. "Jesus will help you."

"Oh, Mother—"

"Have you asked him? Have you asked the Savior to help you?"

"Yes." I hadn't exactly asked him personally. But I thought of the time Daniel had prayed over me, and assumed that counted. "Yes, I have. And Daniel"—I gestured toward the youth minister, sitting in beatific calm across from us—"he laid hands on me and prayed for me. But it didn't work. It didn't work." I hoped that perhaps Mom would take God's lack of immediate action as evidence that the Lord didn't mind. Fat chance.

"And have you prayed every day for help? Every day?"

"No," I had to admit. "Not every day." Not once, actually.

"No?" A look of utter incredulity tilted my mother's face. "And why not? Don't you want to be normal?"

Normal? Didn't I want to be normal? Well, did I? Most days, if you asked me if I really wanted to be anything else than what I was, I'd have probably paused, given the matter a few moments' thought, and said no. But that frightening Saturday night, when my mother asked the musical question "Don't you want to be normal?" all I could think was that I certainly didn't want more of this.

I didn't want my own parents wishing I'd never been born, didn't want them to hurt and cry and think me sick and godless (and tell me so to my face). I couldn't help thinking perhaps it might be better to have your father break your face and get it over with, though I couldn't say I exactly wanted that, either.

But did I want to be normal?

From where I was sitting, the alternative looked unbearable.

Don't you want to be normal?

"I—I guess so."

"You *guess* so?"

"Yes." I finally relented. "Yes, I do."

Dad looked up, his eyes bloody red, and spoke coherently for the first time since I'd come home.

"Of course you do, son. You're no pervert. No son of mine is gonna be a pervert. You're just a little confused, that's all."

Confused? Daddy (I thought), you don't know from confused.

"I'm afraid what we're dealing with here is more serious than just confusion," Daniel said. "I'm convinced that this is a case of possession by unclean spirits."

"What?" Mom, Dad, and I said in chorus.

"You're saying I'm possessed? Like in *The Exorcist?*"

"In a manner of speaking."

"I don't believe that," Mom said with finality.

"Oh, there's any amount of Biblical precedent here." Daniel opened the Bible I have never seen him without and turned quickly to a page marked with a little slip of paper—he'd obviously done some homework. "Book of Mark, chapter five, verse two: 'And when he was come out of the ship, immediately there met him out of the tombs a man with an unclean spirit.' And yudda yudda yudda, verse nine: 'And he asked him, What is thy name? And he answered, saying, My name is Legion: for we are many.'

"And yudda yudda." He moved his finger down the page. "And verse eleven: 'Now there was there nigh unto the mountains a great herd of swine feeding. And all the devils besought him, saying, Send us into the swine, that we may enter into them. And forthwith Jesus gave them leave. And the unclean spirits went out, and entered into the swine.' Also Luke, chapter eight—"

"I don't know about this unclean spirits mess," Mom said, giving me a vigorous version of her trademark finger-wag, "but I know this: you can beat this thing. I know you can. You just. Have. To pray!" Mom punctuated her words with slaps to the top of the coffee table. "Pray. Every day. Read your Bible. Every day." She was beginning to sound like Billy Graham via Daniel Levine. "Trust the Lord to help you. And He *will*, Johnnie Ray. He! Will!"

"Yes." I felt broken, battered, as if I'd just been beat up by a drunken motorcycle gang.

"You just have to give girls a chance, son," my father added. "You just haven't given girls a chance. What about that nice Cherie? I thought for sure you had somethin' nice going with her."

It's what you wanted to think, Daddy. (I thought that to myself, but I didn't dare say it. I could think of nothing whatever to say.)

My God, what was I supposed to do? Somehow make myself want girls the way I just naturally wanted guys? From what I knew on the subject, girls were not supposed to be an acquired taste, like oysters on the half-shell. Daniel says I'm demon-possessed, and Dad says give girls a chance. Give girls a chance, he tells me. All we are say-ing, is give girls a chance. How could anyone think it was that simple?

"I can't do it."

"What?" Mom sat up rigid again; Dad started to sniffle.

"I can't do it alone," I said. "I know I can't. I just can't."

"You won't be alone!" Mom almost screamed it. "Jesus will help you."

"If I may suggest something"—Daniel raised an inquiring index finger—"Johnnie Ray might well be right."

"What?" Mom clutched at her belly again.

"As I've said, this seems to be a clear case of unclean spirits. There are instances—the story of Legion, for example—in which these spirits are so strong, or so numerous, that it is difficult if not impossible for the afflicted to heal himself through prayer; or even for the average minister like myself to help the victim."

"Oh my Jesus," Mom said, "what can we do?"

"I have a friend," said Daniel. "His name is Solomon Hunt, and his spiritual gift is in the deliverance from unclean spirits. He's often able to help where others can't."

"Deliverance from—you're talking about exorcism here, aren't you?" I said. I wasn't sure I liked the direction this conversation was moving in.

"It's similar, I suppose, but—"

"You really think this Solomon could help?" Dad swabbed at his nose with a sopping handkerchief.

"Yes, I do. I've seen him help others. I could set up an appoint-ment with Solomon—"

"When?" Mom.

"As early as, say, tomorrow after church."

"The sooner the better," said Mom.

And that (as they say) was that.

Before Daniel finally took his leave, the four of us joined hands and sang "Yield Not to Temptation."

CHAPTER
20

MONDAY EVENING, THE DAY AFTER my deliverance from unclean spirits, while Mom was washing the dinner dishes (humming "Yield Not to Temptation"), the telephone rang. I was sitting in the living room, pretending to read the newspaper (and I never read the newspaper—too depressing) but actually contemplating my recent past and immediate future. I picked up the phone halfway through the first ring.

"Hello?"

"Don't say anything." Efrem, speaking in a conspiratorial stage whisper. "We have to talk. Sneak out of the house around midnight and meet me at El Taco, okay? If you'll be there, say 'I'm sorry, I'm afraid you have the wrong number.'"

"I'm sorry, I'm afraid you have the wrong number."

"Who's on the phone?" Mom called from the kitchen before the receiver had even left my hand.

"Wrong number."

Luckily, Mom and Dad can always be counted on to be in bed well before ten o'clock. The sound of Dad's snoring filled the house by eleven. Since I had to walk all the way to El Taco, I was glad to have the extra time. The place was practically deserted except for Efrem, who was sitting alone in a back booth sipping a large soft drink. His face was almost back to normal. Except for the fact that he looked as if he hadn't smiled since the Accident, and might in fact never smile again.

"Hi."

He almost smiled when he saw me.

"Sit down. It's good to see you."

"Good to see you, too." I hadn't seen Efrem since I'd left him at the hospital, right after the Accident. He hadn't been back to school in going on three weeks, and after my initial visit to the hospital, Mom and Dad had informed me that maybe it might be better for me not to spend time with Efrem for a while. Just in case homosexuality was contagious, I suppose. I'd called a couple of times, but Efrem's father had answered the phone and said that Efrem was asleep, no matter what time I called.

"You look pretty good," I said.

"All things considered." One side of Efrem's mouth went up, but it wasn't a smile exactly.

"Yeah. How are things at home?"

"Oh, fabulous. My father has neither spoken to me nor looked me in the face since—well, since. And Mom just looks at me as if I've died and she's in mourning. It's a barrel of laughs. In case you haven't heard, I've been officially cured by the power of the Holy Spirit, yuk yuk; but I don't think either of my folks are really buying it."

"Did you get the deliverance treatment, too?"

"No. Daniel prayed over me right there in my hospital room; and after he was finished, I told them it worked, I was cured and I'd go and sin no more. And you know, I think they all wanted to believe it so much that they decided to go ahead and pretend to believe it. I guess now the trick is not to think about it very much. How about you? You got delivered?"

"So they tell me."

"So? Tell."

The waitress came over. She was a girl I knew of but didn't exactly know from school. She dyed her hair red, and was known as something of a slut. I think her name was Gloria something.

"You want something?"

"Who, me? No, not for me, thanks." I'd completely forgotten to bring my wallet. All I had on me was my house key.

"Bring him a large Dr. Pepper, and we'll share a large order of onion rings. On me," he said.

"Thanks. Anyway, about the deliverance."

It wasn't anything like I expected. There were none of the trappings of mystic metaphysics I thought I'd see. No dark rooms with flocks of lighted candles; no incense, no splashing of holy water—well, these were Baptists, after all. It was done in Solomon Hunt's living room in Canoga Park. The afternoon was hot and smoggy and the atmosphere was not in the least bit metaphysical, as far as I could tell.

Neither, in my opinion, was Solomon Hunt himself. Solomon Hunt did not, as I had assumed, look like Max von Sydow in *The Exorcist*. He looked more like Richard Thomas in "The Waltons." He answered the door wearing jeans, a "Maranatha" T-shirt, and no shoes. He looked about the same age as Marshall, and to tell you the truth, he was almost as cute. Not the most encouraging first reaction for a guy who's come to be cured of thinking guys are cute. Daniel had, of course, accompanied Mom, Dad, and me on the two-hour drive to the Hunts' house, and we all sat down as Solomon's wife, a pretty young woman who looked like she could have just as easily been Solomon's sister, asked if anybody wanted coffee. Nobody did.

Daniel made introductions all around, and as I shook Solomon Hunt's hand, I noticed that he had one of the strongest handshakes I'd ever felt, and that his eyes were so light a blue that they almost looked blind, useless; they seemed to look through me and out into nothing at all.

Solomon took both my hands in his.

"Let us pray." He closed his eyes tight. "Lord Jesus"—he held the first syllable of Jesus way out, and bit off the second—"let your blessed Holy Spirit be with us here this day, and give us your precious healing pow-ah. I pray in the name of Jay-zuss. Ayyy-man."

Mom and Dad and Daniel amen'd back. It occurred to me that this Solomon person had watched entirely too many Billy Graham crusades on TV. He had quite a well-developed sense of the dramatic, and an obviously affected in again/out again Boston Clam Chowder accent. I'd walked into this thing with a certain skepticism. I wasn't any too sure I really wanted to be cured of my homosexuality; and I certainly didn't believe this young man (who looked more like a J. C. student than a great Deliverer) could cure me even if I *was* sure I wanted it.

I'd only agreed to come at all out of utter desperation. I knew there was no way I could make myself straight. I like guys. I like liking guys. So if somebody could actually pray me into active heterosexuality, I was willing to let them. It could only make life simpler. I could settle down with Cherie Baker (or someone an awful lot like her) and sire many children. Besides, considering my parents' reaction to the news of what they (wrongly) believed to be unnatural desires as yet not acted upon, what real choice did I have? Unfortunately, I wasn't so sure I was going to be able to keep a straight face through much of Solomon Hunt's Jay-zussing all over the place.

Solomon was squatting in front of the chair where I sat; he pulled me down to the floor with him, directing me to kneel.

"You are possessed of unclean spirits," he said, like the school nurse telling me I had a touch of the flu. "Possession by unclean spirits is not uncommon, and has quite a bit of biblical precedent. In Mark five—"

"Yes," I said. "I've heard."

"Oh. Well, at any rate: with the healing power of the Holy Spirit, we are going to bring those spirits out of your body, out of your soul, and rid you of them, forever. I've done this many times before, so you can feel very confident of success. Now"—he put his hands on my shoulders—"we're going to pray for you—all of us—for your deliverance. It may take a little while; we're prepared to wait as long as it takes. Because Jay-zus wants your soul much more than these unclean spirits do." Solomon's voice was steadily rising in volume, and he was beginning to squeeze my shoulders to an uncomfortable degree. "And the pow-ah of Jayyy-zus is stuh-rong-gah, than any and all unclean spirits. Praise Jay-zus!"

"Praise Jesus," parroted Daniel.

"Now, when the spirits leave your body, they may come out as a sneeze or a coughing spell or something like that. I've had one or two people throw up. But I know these spirits will leave you. By the pow-ah, of Jayyyy-zusss." Solomon shut his eyes again, holding my shoulders in a vise-like grip. "Lord Jayzus," he began, his Billy Graham tribute in full swing, "send us your Holy Spirit here this day; raaaaaain down your healing, yo-wah heaaaaling, pow-ah! And heal, and HEEEEEAL this yo-ah child!"

"Yes, Jesus!" said Daniel.

"Please, my Jesus!" said Mom.

Solomon let go of my shoulders, and took my head into his hands (his long fingers encircling my skull), and gripped it tight, shaking me by the head as he prayed, his voice rising in volume and pitch, his tone growing steadily more urgent, his accent steadily more Eastern: "Lord Jayzus, we pray for your pow-ah, for your great healing POW-ah!"

"Yes, Jesus," repeated Mom, her fists clenched, her face clenched.

"Look down upon us assembled heah this awf-ternoon, and SEND us your great healing pow-ah! Look down on this your child"—he gave my head a particularly vigorous shake—"and

HEAL him! CLEANSE him! Lord God, de-LIV-ah him from the ungodly spiritual forces which hold him . . . CAP-tive, which . . . im-PRI-son him in chains of unnatural . . . de-SI-yahs."

"Hallelujah," shouted Daniel, his palms upturned toward the ceiling.

"All we here gathered acknowledge that thou art God—Hallelujah—and that thou art able (Thank you, Jay-zus) that thou art able to delivah, to DELIVAH this your child, this your servant from the bondage of unclean spirits. Look down upon us, Lord, and have MERCY!"

"Lord, have mercy," whispered Mom.

"Please, Jesus," added Dad.

"Thank you, Jeeezussss," hissed Daniel.

And so it went. For five minutes. For ten. For half an hour; then an hour. And I felt no different, save for a little soreness in my thighs and haunches from kneeling, and in my neck from Solomon shaking my head for a hour. And it was somewhere in the first few minutes of the second hour that I decided to face facts: nothing of any consequence was going to happen here. Because, in the final analysis, I knew I was no more possessed of unclean spirits than the man in the moon. Because, when it came down to brass tacks, I just couldn't seem to bring myself to believe that the God who made me what I am could be any more displeased with me for not being heterosexual than for not being tall. Because, when you got right down to the real nitty-gritty, I didn't really want to be anything other than what I am. And wanting to go straight so Mom and Dad wouldn't cry anymore didn't count.

I looked up at Solomon, his eyes still shut, his hands still tight around my scalp. His boyish brow was crimped with frowns, and he was sweating like a long-distance runner. I knew he was beginning to lose his voice; he could barely rasp, "Please-Jesus-have-mercy" yet another time. I looked at my mother, my father, our hirsute, formerly Jewish youth minister—all of them sweating great drops, squeezing their eyes shut, wringing their hands, and petitioning the Almighty with all their collective might for my deliverance. If it hadn't been me down there on Solomon Hunt's living-room floor, I might have found a certain dark humor in the situation. But it *was* me. And it wasn't funny. I felt sad and cold, and very much alone. And I knew what I had to do.

I screamed.

I sucked in a good long breath and screamed from the top of my falsetto to the bottoms of my feet. I screamed to do Fay Wray proud. The term "blood-curdling" would not have constituted hyperbole.

Needless to say, I stopped the show. Solomon stopped delivering. Mom and Dad and Daniel stopped Hallelujah-ing. Mrs. Hunt emerged from the kitchen, where she'd been keeping herself conveniently busy and out of the way for the entire proceedings. Everybody looked at me. Solomon slid his hands from the top of my head down to my chin, lifted my face to his, and, smiling a John-Boy Walton smile, said:

"That was it, wasn't it?"

"Yes," I said. "That was it."

"And you told them you were cured. Healed, delivered." Efrem poked at the ice at the bottom of his paper cup with the straw.

"I didn't have to. They all assumed my unclean spirits departed my tortured little body in the scream. We all Hallelujah'd and Praise-the-Lorded ourselves into a froth, and sang 'Amazing Grace, How Sweet the Sound,' and went on home."

"And why a scream, if I may ask?"

"I thought it would be more impressive than a coughing spell. And I'll be darned if I was gonna throw up for them. Funny thing: Solomon said my unclean spirits were obviously strong and many, because he usually gets rid of them in less than an hour. Sounded like an exterminator." I chomped into an onion ring.

"Do you suppose your folks really believe you've gone straight?"

"About as much as yours believe you, I guess. I mean, they do and they don't. They want to believe it, of course. They need to, like they need oxygen. But they still look at me like I was a time bomb, about to go off any second."

"I know what you mean. Well"—he clicked the edge of his cup against the counter top—"at least my father hasn't beaten me within inches of my life lately. He hasn't looked me in the eye in recent memory, either, but them's the breaks. God, I've got to get out of there. Barmaid!" He waved his empty cup in the air as a signal for a refill.

"I know. I can't wait till the fall."

"I don't intend to wait that long, if I can help it."

"What do you mean?"

"I mean I'm leaving this ass-kissin' burg, and soon. John and I are gonna move to San Francisco. It's supposed to be gay heaven up there."

"You're not even gonna finish school?"

"Maybe, maybe not. Depends on when John decides it's time to hit the road. I know damn well I'm not hangin' around *here* all summer long." Efrem stared into the onion rings while Gloria deposited another 7-Up and left. He tried to speak up at the exact moment I tried to speak up.

"I'm sorry," I said. "Go ahead."

"No, you go ahead."

"It's rather personal."

"Hey, you've just given me the blow-by-blow of your exorcism, for cryin' out loud. Heaven forbid we should get personal."

"All right, then. About John: are you in love with him?"

"No," he said with little hesitation. "Not really. He's kind and sweet, just a basic nice guy. Not great-looking, but nice-looking. I like him a lot, and I like . . . you know, being in bed with him and all, but—see, ever since I was a little kid, I've had this dream of meeting a guy, a certain guy, and falling in love and setting up housekeeping with him, and living happily ever after, like in the movies. And I still think that guy is out there someplace, and I'll find him. Or he'll find me.

"And I'm pretty sure I'll know that guy, practically on sight. You know, I'll just feel something. 'Some Enchanted Evening' and all that. Anyway, John isn't that guy. Just isn't. But, like I said, I do like him, and he's nuts about me, don't ask me why. And he'll get me out of here."

I was about to tell Efrem all about Marshall, everything, in detail—I didn't know where in the world to start—when Efrem said, "May I ask you something personal now?"

"Sure. I guess you're entitled."

"I don't believe I'm really going to ask you this." Efrem rolled his eyes ceilingward, then leaned forward and whispered, "Are you attracted to me?"

That took me back a step. I'd hardly even thought of Efrem in sexual terms before. I've always thought he was good-looking, in that pale, big-eyed, bookish sort of way he has; but sexually? I quickly revised Efrem's question in my mind, asking myself if I would consider making love with Efrem Zimbalist Johnson; to which the answer was an unequivocal yes. I liked and cared for Efrem, and while that wasn't exactly the same as having the four-alarm hots for him, I decided it was close enough that I could say, "Yes. As a matter of fact, I am." Efrem smiled. He didn't smile all that often during the best of times (his wonted facial expression is more of a mid-range smirk), which is a shame, since he is most handsome when he smiles.

"Then I can admit I've had a crush on you practically since we first met."

"You're kidding. Me?"

"Yes, you. Not everybody loves the blonds, you know."

"Oh, really? And what blonds are we discussing here?"

"Okay, fine: play it coy. Do the names Skipper Harris and Todd

Waterson mean anything?" He suddenly sobered at the mention of Todd.

I'd felt a certain sinking of the stomach at the mention of Todd's name, but I decided it was best to keep it light.

"Was I that obvious?"

"I wasn't sure, of course. Cherie threw me off totally. But, in light of recent events, a lot of behavior starts to make sense. And, while we're on the subject, what about Cherie?"

"Cherie knows. She's known almost from the beginning. Her and Skipper."

"Skipper?"

"Oh, yes, and some snowy night by the fire I'll regale you with that little saga. I've got lots to tell you"—I was simply itching to talk about Marshall—"but not tonight. I'm so sleepy."

Efrem leaned forward across the table and whispered, "Do you want to come home with me?"

"What? Spend the night? Are you nuts?"

"No. I could sneak you in through the window. I really want you to."

"I want to, too." And I really did. The thought of holding Efrem in my arms after all this time, of seeing and feeling what my buddy was like all naked and hard, was intriguing, at the very least. "But I'd be too scared to risk it. And I should think you'd be too. You haven't got the best history of sneaking people in and out of bedroom windows."

Efrem blanched.

"I'm sorry." I reached out and touched Efrem's hand, then quickly pulled back. "Really."

"S'okay. Well, you cannot claim I never offered you the riches of my small but wiry body. Maybe next time. We better go, huh? It's practically dawn."

We ambled over to the register.

"Are you coming back to school tomorrow?" I asked.

Efrem shrugged. "Maybe."

As soon as we got out the door, I had an idea. I grabbed Efrem by the arm and led him toward the back of the building, out by the dumpsters. It was almost pitch-dark back there, and it stank with the sort of acrid stink peculiar to decaying junk food.

"Jeez, Johnnie Ray, what're you trying to do? Make me sick?"

"We won't be long," I said, leading him back behind the piled-high dumpsters, where I was sure we would be completely obscured from the view of any who might pass by. I took Efrem in my arms, and we held each other tight for a long moment. Then kissed, softly and tenderly, on the lips.

"Be happy, Efrem."

"You, too, Johnnie Ray."

CHAPTER
21

EFREM DID INDEED RETURN TO school the next morning; he and Cherie and I were at the old stand in the choir room at a quarter to eight, pretty much as per usual. I would have expected Efrem to be treated to a few prying questions from our classmates—some rude, searching stares at the very least. But no. It seemed to be business as usual around the choir room. I suppose what with the semester drawing to a close all around us, and final exams, commencement exercises, and Life itself lying just over the next hill, Efrem's accident was yesterday's news.

When I asked Efrem how he was doing, he shrugged and said,

"Okay, I guess." Then he sighed a long deep sigh and said, "I can't wait to get out of here," like a man just this side of stir-crazy.

"Do you know when you're going?" I asked as we sat on the Drama-room porch during lunch hour.

"Soon," he said; and I could tell he really didn't know when (maybe even *if*) he was leaving, but was hoping to God on high it would be soon. I knew the feeling well. I also knew that, in the final analysis, Efrem would be all right. If he ended up hanging around long enough, he'd graduate, probably with his usual 3.8 GPA intact; and if not, he'd still get along. Efrem was just altogether too sharp not to.

As for me, I'd gone underground, after a fashion. I still lived with my parents, but I avoided them whenever possible. I'd always been one for spending most of my time in my room with my books and my records and my macramé for company; now, if anything, I spent even more time alone than ever, venturing out only infrequently and briefly, for meals and the bathroom. When I did see Mom and Dad, the sense of being watched, studied—the infinitely uncomfortable feeling of being under surveillance—was next to unbearable. During dinner, I'd look up from my peas and carrots to find Dad peering intently at me over the meat loaf; or Mom would say, "Have you read your Bible today?" while staring a hole through me, and I'd find it difficult to swallow my food. It's not so easy on the nerves, feeling like a time bomb.

So, as I said, I went underground. I went to school and studied and kept pretty much to myself. I was already beginning to count the days, not only until graduation, but until what was certain to be the longest, hottest, most uncomfortable summer of my life had come and gone. Until I, too, could be gone.

About a week after Efrem came back, about a week before finals, I think it was a Wednesday night, I was awakened by the unmistakable sound of a motorcycle coming up our driveway. I had fallen asleep sprawled across my bed with my face in my trig book—the last thing I remembered was staring blankly into the book, wondering half-aloud what possible use a logarithm might be in my future life, when suddenly I heard this motorcycle in front of the house.

Now, this isn't a big motorcycle town. It's a Chevy-van town, a souped-up Toyota-truck town. There just aren't that many motorbikes around here. So when I heard the cycle outside, I immediately thought, Todd. It had to be Todd. At my house. I literally jumped out of bed, my heart thumping, and did a double-time tippy-toe run down the hall and through the living room, and opened the front door just as Todd Waterson's Honda Three-Sixty sputtered to a stop in the driveway. I watched Todd dismount and kick-stand the bike, and pushed open the screen door to let him in.

"Todd," I whispered.

"Hello, Johnnie Ray." Todd was talking as if it were high noon instead of after midnight. I ran to close the hall door between the living room and my parents' room.

"My folks are asleep."

"Sorry."

"It's good to see you. Where in the world have you been? Are you okay? What are you doing here?" To my memory, Todd had never been to our house before—I wouldn't have thought he knew the address. Here he'd been gone—missing, in fact—for the better part of five weeks, and suddenly, in the middle of the night, he pops up at my house. It made no sense.

He looked terrible. His hair was visibly dirty and matted with grease; his jeans and T-shirt and Levi's jacket were so dirty and wrinkled, it was a foregone conclusion that he'd been sleeping in them, probably for as long as he'd been away. And as he stepped into the house, I realized he smelled worse than he looked. I took a step back in an attempt to escape the funk.

"I just came to say goodbye," he said.

"Goodbye? You've been gone for weeks, and now you're saying goodbye? Where are you going? Where have you been?"

"I just wanted to let you know what a good Christian brother you've been to me."

"Where have you *been*, Todd? Do your folks know you're back?"

"No." He grabbed me by the arm, squeezing hard. "And don't you tell them you saw me. Just don't, okay?"

"Okay. Okay." He let go of my arm.

"Anyway, I know what you've been doing, and I appreciate it."

"What have I been doing?"

"You know: being nice to me when everybody else was treating me like shit. Being my friend. The song and everything. Sorry I won't be able to do it with you."

"So stay and do it with me. Stay till after the concert." There was something wrong here. But really wrong. I wasn't sure just what was going on in Todd's matty blond head, but I felt like I should hang on to him, not let him go wherever it was he thought he was going. I knew I couldn't stall him there forever, but I didn't know what else to do. Todd shook his head.

"No. No, I gotta go. Like I said, I just wanted to say thanks. Say goodbye." I was at a complete loss for what to do. I stammered a few syllables, reached out to touch Todd's shoulder, and stopped short, then stammered a little more.

"I also wanted to give you this." Todd pulled the silver-and-opal ring off his little finger (the ease with which it slipped off made me notice just how much thinner Todd was than when I'd seen him last; I wondered when he'd last eaten). He held the ring out in his dirty palm. The sight of that nearly knocked the wind right out of me.

I suddenly knew, as if informed by a reliable source, what Todd planned to do. Even without my on-again off-again intuition, even if Todd and I hadn't joked that I'd get the ring Leslie gave him only over his dead body, any Psych 1 student knows what it means when somebody who's been through some major-league personal loss starts giving away his prized possessions. I don't think I'd ever felt such horror.

I pushed Todd's hand away.

"No. Keep it. You'll want it yourself." My voice had jumped a nervous octave. I glanced toward the hall door (I could hear Dad's snoring all the way from the bedroom), wondering if I shouldn't wake up my folks.

"Please take it." Todd thrust his hand out toward me. "I want you to have it."

"Please, Todd," I said, beginning to feel desperation clutching at my throat. "Take the ring. Don't go—wherever you're going, don't go. Just go home, Todd." I clutched at the collar of Todd's jacket. "Please go home."

"I've got to go now." Todd took my hand, placed the ring firmly in the center of my palm, and closed my fingers around it.

"Please!" I was beginning to cry. I looked into Todd's face, he was smiling.

"I've got to go now," he repeated. He gathered me into a big hug. He held me tight against his foul-smelling chest, so tight it hurt my ribs, and said, "I love you in Jesus."

Then he released me, turned and let himself out the screen door, mounted his bike, and was gone. Leaving me standing at my front door, feeling small and powerless and scared. Staring through the screen door with Todd's ring tight in my fist, and tears falling down my face.

Finally, suddenly, as the sound of Todd's bike faded away, I ran toward my parents' bedroom, screaming like the eyewitness to a murder: "Mom! Dad! Wake up!"

About ten miles out of town, due north, is a steep, narrow winding mountain road known as Grady Pass. It is one of the sillier traditions around here that, on the last day of Driver's Training, at least one lucky (or unlucky, as you prefer) student driver brave that hill-hugging road, curling precariously above the valley, in one of the school's Ford Pintos. It has long been an event of squealing anticipation for girls, a thrill-seeking macho rite of passage for the kind of thick-necked male type given to such things, to clutch and brake one's way up one side of Grady Pass and down the other, arriving back at school with one's instructor, one's back-seat-driving classmates, and one's ass in one piece. A couple of years back, a fun-loving home ec class even designed an "I Survived Grady Pass" T-shirt, to be presented to each successful driver at the end of his ordeal.

It is, naturally, local legend that at least one carful of students (and their teacher) met an untimely end attempting to navigate Grady Pass. No one seems to know exactly who these unfortunate students might have been, nor when this misfortune may have occurred. The worst case that can be remembered personally by anyone I know is that now and then a student (generally female) goes somewhat hysterical halfway up the Pass, forcing the instructor to assume the driver's seat. Still, a legend's a legend; and in a town like this one, even a half-assed legend is better than none.

There is, therefore, a mystique surrounding Grady Pass such as smallish towns all over America love to attach to such local landmarks as the creek where the mousy bespectacled bank teller deliberately drowned his wife of twenty-seven years; the tree where they once hanged an innocent man by mistake; or the broken-down old house where lives the old man who frightens the neighbor kids, eats kitty-cats for supper, and allows his front lawn to burn brown in the summertime.

And so, it was with a certain amount of awe and barely concealed excitement mixed with the expected horror and sadness that the word traveled from mouth to mouth like a cold sore, as telephones buzzed with the news that on that Wednesday evening (probably mere minutes after giving me both his precious opal ring and the tightest hug I'd ever felt) Todd Waterson had driven his Honda Three-Sixty motorcycle over the edge at Grady Pass, snapping his neck and dying almost instantly on impact with the valley below.

As Grady Pass is very seldom used for anything other than Driver's Training (and not all that often for that), there were no witnesses to the spectacle of the motorcycle sailing over the embankment; Todd had been dead nearly two full days before the police and paramedics managed to get down to him, separate what was left of Todd from what was left of the Honda, and deliver the broken remains of what a scant forty-eight hours earlier had been perhaps the most beautiful boy in town, to the morgue.

I cried uncontrollably Saturday morning when Mom told me; she'd just gotten the news from good old reliable Hildy Brooks that Todd was indeed dead, that Mrs. Waterson was beside herself and was under sedation. She looked at me, wearing that confused, somewhat tormented look she seemed to wear so much lately, then turned quickly away, murmuring "Lord, have mercy today." I sobbed aloud, sitting against the stereo in my bedroom, banging my head against the cabinet; I cried until my throat was sore, until I had no tears left. I cried out of a bitter mixture of emotions, sorrow included, but not sorrow alone.

My initial reaction to the news of Todd's suicide was, in fact, guilt. Why hadn't I stopped Todd from going when the idea of his killing himself came to me, whispered in the wee small voice people like to talk about? Couldn't I have stopped him? And then I thought: even if I'd fallen into a trance at the sound of Todd's Honda in the driveway, and seen his impending death in a Technicolor vision, what could I really have done to stop him? Talk him out of it? Wrestle him to the ground? Hog-tie him?

What I did do, of course—after Todd had already driven away—was wake up Mom and Dad.

"Dad!" I shook my loudly snoring father sputteringly awake. "Dad, Todd Waterson was just here, and I think he's gonna kill himself!"

Mom woke, raised herself up on one elbow, grabbed a handful of her sleep-flattened Afro, and asked the ceiling, "Lord, have mercy, where is the end?"

"What?" Dad thrust his face close to mine—he had that bad breath he always has upon awakening. "Did he tell you that?"

"No," I had to admit. "It's just a feeling."

Todd's sudden reappearance was in itself enough to get Mom and Dad out of bed and into their bathrobes. We called the Watersons'—the line was busy—and then the police. Sergeant Crandall (the Pastor's younger brother) arrived in record time. The sergeant got all the looks in the family, he looked like Robert Taylor in *Camille* and filled a cop uniform like nobody I'd ever seen. He questioned me closely but, like my folks, was obviously hesitant to take the suicide notion very seriously, simply because Todd never actually *told* me he was going to do it—even after I explained about the ring, and showed it to him, to boot. I was outraged: Did policemen no longer believe in hunches?

The sergeant assured us all that Todd could not have gotten very far and would be found, and that he would personally go to the Watersons and alert them to the situation. Then he suggested we get some sleep. Strangely, sleep came quickly for me—quickly, and mercifully dreamless.

It was not, in fact, until Friday night, at nearly three in the morning, that I suddenly awoke out of a sound sleep, in a sweat and breathing hard. I jumped out of bed, literally ran to the telephone, and called the police.

"Night desk," a voice answered.

And I said, "Grady Pass."

My second reaction was anger. How dare he kill himself? How could this tall and blond and almost obscenely beautiful young man take his own life? He had no right. Even granted the fact that he'd just lost the one person on earth he seemed to give a damn about, he simply had no right. Leslie's death was a waste; Todd's was waste on waste. As Mom said, where was the end?

Finally, after what seemed like years of tears, thought, and self-questioning, a strange sort of peace came upon me. Hardly peace like a river, but maybe a brook. As I said, I finally decided I couldn't blame myself for Todd's death. I'd done what I could do. And if my psychic abilities were inconsistent and late, well, that wasn't exactly my fault, either. It also occurred to me that, wherever Todd was, he was probably with Leslie—which, I'm sure, was exactly what he wanted. I have no idea where such a notion could have sprung from. It went against everything I knew from church. In fact, much of the grief exhibited by Mom and Dad and the other parents stemmed from the belief that, having taken their own lives, both Leslie and Todd were (for now and eternity) burning in hell. Well, no way was I buying any of that Crazy World of Arthur Brown everlasting hellfire hoo-ha. Couldn't *make* myself believe that one.

But the thought that Leslie and Todd were together again, on some plane of existence somewhere, was infinitely attractive to me, and it stuck in my mind like a wad of Double-Bubble in a little girl's hair.

I got into bed, lay back and closed my eyes, and tried to imagine another world, another planet maybe, where Todd and Leslie could have just had their baby without the whole world grinding to a halt. Where Efrem wouldn't have to fear his own father. Where I could relax and just be me.

I didn't go to Todd's funeral. I knew most of the old youth-group gang would be there, the same kids who wouldn't give Todd directions to the drugstore when he was alive. And I knew there was no way on earth I was going to deal with that kind of hypocrisy in that kind of volume. Besides, it wasn't as if Todd and I were these big Damon and Pythias buds, exactly. My only problem was what to do with Todd's ring. I just didn't feel I should keep it, despite how much I liked it, notwithstanding his wanting me to have it. I couldn't bring myself to wear it, anyway. It sat in the little trinket box I'd made in eighth-grade shop, among my old Beatles buttons and the genuine hippie love beads somebody gave me when I was ten.

Finally, on the afternoon of Todd's funeral, I put the ring into a plain white business-size envelope, hopped on my bike, and pedaled over to the Watersons'. I dropped the envelope in the mailbox. And said goodbye to Todd one last time.

CHAPTER

22

THE SPRING CONCERT WAS HELD in the gym (as usual), since we have no auditorium. The bleachers were down on one side (for the audience) and up on the other (in lieu of a stage). All the choir girls wore formals for the performance and the guys all rented white dinner jackets, which made us look like a mass prom portrait. Mom bought me a red carnation boutonniere, and Dad insisted upon snapping picture after picture of me and Cherie (a vision in blue chiffon). I hadn't gone to my junior or senior prom—I'd wanted to take Skipper, and both times he already had a date—and I guess Mom and Dad wanted the pictures as some sort of consolation prize.

It was nice to look out into the bleachers and see those of the Drama II gang who weren't also in choir. Skipper was there—wrapped half-way around Kathleen as usual, but that really didn't bug me anymore. Also Crystal, wearing a big smile and a mini-skirt cut up to *there*, and absolutely festooned with costume jewelry. Somewhere inside her, Carolann was probably dying of embarrassment. It would have been perfect if Marshall had somehow miraculously been there; but hey, life isn't exactly perfect, is it?

The concert itself went pretty well, considering nervousness and the fact that we're hardly the world's greatest high-school choir at the best of times. The interludes came right after intermission; and, naturally, I nearly tossed my cookies waiting for my turn. Johnny and Janie Foley sang and strummed a two-handed version of "If I Had a Hammer" à la Peter Paul and Mary. They were good, and the applause was good, too. Johnny stayed on to play guitar for me, and when I walked on Mom said "Go 'head, Baby," from the audience, and there were some laughs. That helped me break through my nervousness; I said "Thanks, Mom" into the microphone, and there were some more laughs. Johnny kicked into the intro to "Blackbird," and I raised my hand to stop him.

"I'd like to dedicate this song," I said, "to absent friends." Even though I couldn't see anybody because of the spotlight, I could hear shiftings in the bleachers, and somebody said a long descending "Oh." I signaled Johnny to begin, closed my eyes, and sang.

When I was finished, and Johnny had plucked the last notes of the accompaniment from his guitar, there was a long moment of silence. You could have heard a Q-Tip drop. I did hear my heartbeat. Then the applause, like a storm. Clapping and whistling and screaming and stomping on the bleachers. Somebody called "More!" I turned to Johnny Foley, who was backing out of the spotlight, applauding me. I was, to put it mildly, overwhelmed. I just stood there, grinning like the village half-wit, for who knows how long.

"Bow!" Mr. Elmgreen called from the sidelines. "Bow, Johnnie

Ray, bow!" So I did. Forward and right and left and forward again. And still they applauded. And I was smiling and crying, and I bowed in every direction on the compass again, up and down and up and down, like a bobbing birdie toy, and then I ran into Cherie's arms, still smiling, still crying.

I knew right then that this—singing, performing—was something I wanted to do for the rest of my life. The movie of my life was a musical.

CHAPTER

23

AS IT TURNED OUT, EFREM ENDED up graduating with the class, after all—seems his friend John decided that was best. Several of the Drama II gang (and Efrem) went down to the toy store before the commencement exercises and bought enormous pairs of toy sunglasses and wore them all through the ceremony, even going up to get our diplomas. Silly, I guess, but fun. In addition to my oversized shades, I also carried a bouquet of long-stemmed red roses, given to me by Cherie, God love her. I felt like Miss America, only prettier.

Afterward, I made a big point of walking up to Mr. Brock and shaking his hand; I smiled real big and fed him a big line about what an excellent Drama teacher he was and what a rewarding experience it had been working with him and blah blah blah. He looked at me somewhat warily, probably half expecting me to whip a blackjack out of the sleeve of my gown and go upside his head with it.

"Well," he said, "good luck in college, Rouss. And be careful at that U.C.L.A. I hear there's a lot of perverts out there."

"I know," I said, tickling the old fool's palm with my middle finger. "That's why I'm going." Brock blanched white as Wonder Bread and snatched his hand back like I was on fire. I just smiled.

Mom and Dad looked as natural and at ease with me as I'd seen them in many a week. They were both smiling so big I thought their faces might snap, and Dad shook my hand and said, "We're very proud of you, son" about a dozen times. It was a welcome break from the mutual discomfort we'd been feeling lately.

Efrem's mother was at the ceremonies, but not his dad. He'd pleaded an overwhelming backlog of work at his insurance office. I could scarcely believe it—his only son's graduation. Efrem seemed strangely unmoved by his father's pointed no-show, and I understood it better by and by, when a beat-up blue Rambler drove up the narrow street behind the football field and beeped it's horn (a wimpy little beep reminiscent of Marshall MacNeill's dilapidated Saab).

Efrem ran toward me, his gown flapping around him, calling my name. "Come here"—he grabbed me by the arm—"I want you to meet somebody." Efrem ran to the parked Rambler, and I followed him, nearly tripping on my gown.

A tall, well-groomed black man unfolded himself out of the Rambler and walked around the front of the car toward me and Efrem, smiling a fluorescent smile.

"Johnnie Ray Rousseau," Efrem introduced, "John Walker. John, Johnnie Ray." I took John Walker's big hand, and we traded hellos. He looked to be about Marshall's age, maybe a little older. He turned to Efrem.

"You about ready to go?"

"Just about."

"You're going?" I said. "To San Francisco, you mean?"

"That's right." Efrem was smiling like I don't believe I'd ever seen him smile before. Here was one happy young man. "I'll be right back," he said to John, and ran back to where his mother stood with Mom and Dad, all three of them staring out toward the street where John's car waited.

"Well, Mother," Efrem said, "I guess this is goodbye."

"Goodbye?" Mrs. Johnson looked at her son, incredulous and puzzled, as if Efrem had suddenly burst into a foreign language.

"Yes," said Efrem, still smiling, oozing self-assurance from every pore. "Goodbye. I'm going away. I'll be setting up house-keeping elsewhere."

"What are you talking about?" Mrs. Johnson touched at her face, as if afraid it might be slipping out of place. "You can't just leave, just like that."

"That's where you're wrong, Mother. I'm eighteen now. I can do as I like. And for the first time in my life, that's exactly what I'm doing. Now, are you going to kiss me goodbye and wish me luck, or are you gonna stand here and try to tell me what I can and cannot do?"

"Efrem—" She attempted to protest, and Efrem threw his arms around his mother's neck, and kissed her face.

"Goodbye, Mother. I'll get in touch once I'm settled. Take care of yourself. Tell Dad I said toodle-oo, if you think about it." And he was running again, back toward John's Rambler, calling "Come on" over his shoulder.

I turned to Mom and Dad. "I'll be right back, okay?" And I started off after Efrem. I could just hear Mrs. Johnson call Efrem's name, loudly, her voice full of tears.

"All right, let's get out of this burg," Efrem called to John. He stopped at the car and turned to me. "Well, I guess this is it."

"I guess it is." I blinked back tears. I was going to feel very much alone over the summer without Efrem. "You take care of yourself," I said. "You take care of him," I called into the car. Efrem and I hugged each other tight.

"Be happy, Johnnie Ray."

"You too, Efrem."

John opened the passenger door, and Efrem went to climb in, still wearing his graduation gown, the mortarboard askew on his head.

"Haven't you forgotten something?"

Laughing, he ripped open the Velcro fasteners on the gown, dropped it off his shoulders and tossed it at me, then hurled the cap over my head like a Frisbee.

"Bye," Efrem said as John shoved the Rambler into gear.

"Auf wiedersehn," I said. "We'll meet again."

I waved goodbye from the sidewalk, Efrem's graduation gown over my arm, until all that was left of the blue Rambler was the long gray cloud of exhaust that followed it around the corner.

CHAPTER
24

I WRITE THIS FROM THE GAY STU-dents' Union office at U.C.L.A., sitting on a big old chenille sofa between the long outstretched legs (and leaning against the T-shirted chest) of a new buddy of mine. His name is Rod. He looks like a young balding Mick Jagger, and there's an erect, ejaculating phallus embroiderd in Day-Glo colors on the left thigh of his jeans. He's reached up under my arms and is stroking my chest through my shirt, making my handwriting jump a little on the lines. Rod and I haven't slept together or anything; he's just a handsy kind of guy, and frankly, I don't mind.

So, as you may have gathered, I did survive the summer, and I did make it here to the big U. The summer at home was like three months of nonstop itching. I couldn't wait to get out. I spent almost the entire three months in my room, just staying out of sight as much as possible. Some of the time I was with Cherie, watching television and knotting macramé plant-hangers, mostly. And I worked for a while assisting a house painter. But most often I was alone. I got through it.

College doesn't seem substantially different from high school, except that you don't have to go to class if you don't want to; and there's no dress code here—guys come to class in shorts and tank-tops (talk about distracting). And I'm away from home at last. Not miles and miles away, of course; but far enough away, going to a school that's almost as big as the town I left. I like the size, the bigness of this school. I can get lost here if I want to. And I don't just mean not being able to find my classes, though heaven knows I had some of that at first. It's just that there are so many people here, there's no way anybody really gives a flying you-know-what who this Johnnie Ray Rousseau might be or what he might be doing. And I like that. I've never felt so free in my life.

My dorm roommate is a guy named Tom, and he's from Cincinnati. He's blond and frizzy-haired (kind of Art Garfunkly), and I was pretty sure we'd get along when I saw the size of his record collection (it takes up almost his whole side of the room, that and his stereo system). Tom is one of the funniest, wittiest people I've ever met—makes Efrem Zimbalist Johnson look like an autistic child. I was pretty sure Tom was gay our first Monday together, practically at first sight. I was totally sure the following evening, when we both left the room at the same time, and wound up (quite independently) at the first Gay Students' Union meeting of the new term.

That meeting was like the world's biggest homecoming for me. There were over one hundred people there, mostly guys, all shapes and sizes and hues, and all of them gay. I nearly cried just walking in and seeing that. It was sort of a get-to-know-each-other night, and we mostly just talked. Mostly about growing up gay wherever it was we grew up, and how wonderful it was being in a room full of other gays, most of us for the very first time.

Afterward, a bunch of us adjourned to the Parasol, a coffee shop in Westwood Village, where we slurped sundaes and flirted with the busboys. I felt like this must be heaven.

I spent that night with a big, good-looking leather-jacketed law student named Glenn, and it was nice, except that, even as Glenn held me, I couldn't help thinking of Marshall MacNeill.

I got a postcard from Marshall a couple of days ago. I was in the middle of my daily hike uphill to the dorm after University Chorus, when suddenly I thought, I'm going to hear from Marshall (I'm still not moving large objects with my mind, but I do find I'm getting more and more of these little hunches). And lo and behold, there it was, all alone in my little mail slot: a picture postcard of the main drag of a teeny-weeny town, little more than a Texaco station and a post office, with a crystal-blue cloudless sky above it. And across the sky, in big white letters, it said THIS IS VAN HORN.

The postmark was smeared, but I could see it had been stamped in El Paso, sometime in July. Marshall had drawn little five-pointed stars around the address: "Johnnie Ray Rousseau, Student, University of California, Los Angeles." It was a miracle it ever found its way to me at all. It read:

> Jukebox selections in Van Horn's Sands Café include Earth, Wind & Fire, Elton John, and Dobie Gray singing "Drift Away." Anti-nudists in Massachusetts maintain that nudity is contributing to the erosion of the sand dunes in Cape Cod—Channel 3 Evening News, Phoenix. Temp 105 in Phoenix; 106 in El Paso. I'm having walking nightmares listening to what the gov't is doing with nuclear energy. Thanks for coming to my film. I'm working on a letter to you. Marshall.

I've been using the postcard as a bookmark for my French textbook, and taking it with me everywhere.

There's a radio on the old metal desk across the office from Rod and me. Right now, Dobie Gray is singing "Drift Away."

You couldn't slap this smile off my face.